MW01612838

The a novel

TRAINER

Just give me tonight.

SHEY STAHL

USA Today Bestselling Author

Copyright © 2014 by Shey Stahl

Published in the United States of America

ISBN-13: 978-1502499240

ISBN-10: 150249924X

Boxing terms are copyright of: http://www.ringsidebygus.com/boxing-terms.html

"I hated every minute
of training, but I
said, I don't quit.
Suffer now and live
the rest of your life
as a champion."

Muhammad Ali

Table of Contents

Chapter One

Chapter Two

Chapter Three

Chapter Four

Chapter Five

Chapter Six

Chapter Seven

Chapter Eight

Chapter Nine

Chapter Ten

Chapter Eleven

Chapter Twelve

Chapter Thirteen

Chapter Fourteen

Chapter Fifteen

Chapter Sixteen

Chapter Seventeen

Chapter Eighteen

Acknowledgements

About the Author

Chapter One
FIGHT CARD

A fight card or card is a program of boxing consisting of all the boxing matches that take place during a boxing event. Fight cards consist of a main event and an undercard of the rest of the matches.

Monday
April 4, 2011

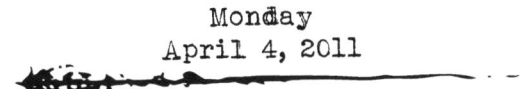

No one uses their home phone anymore. We use cell phones. So when one rings, what do we do?

We stare at it like it's a bomb.

"Phone's for you."

"For me?" I looked at the device like I wasn't sure how to even handle it.

Jared tipped the phone toward me, his other hand bringing his beer to his lips. "Anyone else around? Yes, you."

No one called me anymore unless it was Jared. He can't text for shit so he calls. And he was sitting next to me, so it wasn't him.

I took the phone from him, more than curious as to who was calling me. "Hello?"

There was a distant hum on the other line before a raspy voice asked, "Tallan?"

"Yes…"

Another long pause before, "It's Silas."

"Silas who?"

He chuckled, damn near offended. "Cade… I'm sure you remember, yes?"

Holy. Fucking. Shit.

Immediately I stood and tried to get myself into a more private part of the small apartment. Wasn't really possible so I huddled in the corner between the cabinets and the fridge.

If it wouldn't have been so inappropriate, I would have squealed knowing who was on the other line. And then I would have called the person a liar. Which I'm about to. Just wait.

"No way, is this some sort of April Fool's shit someone's playing on me?"

"Are you calling me a liar?"

See?

"Yes. Because the Silas Cade I know is all over the radio these days and wouldn't be calling his high school fuckbuddy he hasn't spoken to in over five years."

You see, I know one Silas Cade and he's the boy who at sixteen, owned my fucking heart. He also ripped it out when he left two years later to follow his dreams of having a music career.

"Oh come on. You were more than a fuckbuddy, honey."

I didn't say anything to that. I wasn't sure what to say at that point. I was just dumbfounded he was even calling me.

"I know it's been a while but I'm gonna be on tour in Seattle in six weeks. You still live there?"

"Yeah… "

"Would you want to meet up after the concert? I can get you a backstage pass."

Seriously? Like… *seriously*?

Without thinking, I answered. "Sure."

"Really?"

"I could change my mind."

He laughed, the light sound ringing through the line. A smile tugged at my lips. He always had such a beautiful laugh. "Okay, so I'll be in touch then." He sighed slightly, as if he forgot to say something important. "The concert is May eighteenth at the Key Arena."

"Okay." It's so hard to believe that he was playing at venues like that. And even harder to believe that I owned every song he released.

"Bye, Tallan." His raspy voice rang through, so perfect and clear when he said my name. The way the sound rolled off his tongue made me want to beg him to say it again.

Don't say bye. Just stay here on the phone with me forever.

"Bye."

What the hell just happened?

When I set the phone down I wasn't sure what to think about what just happened.

As shitty as it was, Silas still owned my heart and I'd do anything to be with him again. Anything. I knew it wouldn't go anywhere. I have gotten wiser at twenty-two years old but it was, after all, Silas Cade and if I had just one night to show him a good time, that could potentially bring him back, right?

"Who was it?"

I gave Jared a look, one he knew well. "You remember Silas, right?"

"You mean the virgin stealer who broke your heart and is now a famous rock star?" He pointed to the radio. "The guy singing that song? *That guy?*"

I nodded, listening to the sexy rhythm strumming through the radio. "Yes. *That guy.*"

"Nope." He looked back at the television trying to find that show *Naked and Alone.* "Can't recall who that is, actually."

"Well," I sat down next to him on the couch, "the one and only Silas Cade, love of my life is coming back into town and wants to meet up with me… ME!" An inner grin, hell, a fucking outer grin, lighting up my entire face as I told Jared my news.

"Yeah, that sounds about right. Because there's not any other groupies available in Seattle that night?" A look passing over his face that reeked of disapproval. He knew what this was and wasn't sugarcoating it. "A one night booty call at his old stomping grounds… yeah, this has life-long commitment written all over it."

"Shut up, Jared. Don't rain on my Silas Cade parade."

Rolling my eyes, I set the phone on the table in front of us, trying to calm my breathing a little. It'd been so long since I heard from him I wasn't sure how to react. Well, my mind didn't know how to react but my body, just hearing that melt your panties right off your body voice of his, had its own mind and was doing all sorts of funny things at the moment.

Oh. My. God. My body! It wasn't in the same shape as it was five years ago. Twenty pounds heavier and this God of Rock was expecting to see the *old Tallan* with the smoking body. He'd be expecting that girl he left. The one with the long lean legs and flat stomach. Definitely not this girl with the little tummy roll and the flabby legs. We won't talk about the arms and ass just yet.

Six weeks... six weeks to get back into the condition that Silas remembered. Panic was starting to set in right in front of Jared. There was no way in hell I was going to freak out in front of him. I didn't need his sidelong glances of judgment raining down on me. Six weeks, I can do this. Challenge. Fucking. Accepted.

So while I had the idea that I was going to look the same I decided to sneak into my bedroom when Jared turned the TV to the History Channel. Apparently he couldn't find *Naked and Alone*. Guess he was going to content watching *Ice Road Truckers* instead.

I had met Silas when I was only thirteen. We were the same age, even shared a birthday. Over summer break when we were going from the seventh to the eighth grade, we formed a friendship over Pearl Jam. It became our one thing we always went back to. Silas played the guitar and sang but never gave it much thought until I pushed him a little. He had an unbelievable talent and it was evident early on it he wanted a career in music, he would have it.

Eventually him and his friends formed a band. They played all around Seattle in any bar that would let them in. They say it only takes one hit to get you noticed and that was true for Silas. After he left for New York, four months later, his first single, the one he said he wrote for me, "Never Knew" was on the Billboard 100.

Was I depressed when he left?

Fuck yeah I was depressed. I was there for him through everything.

The band drama, his occasional mix up with drugs, his parents splitting up, his sister dying, all of it.

And what did he offer me?

A fucking phone call.

I thought I would never move on. And given the chance, I was going to get my answer.

Going to that concert could potentially give me that opportunity.

Digging through my closet and the box that hadn't been opened since I moved into this apartment, I found my old jeans from high school.

Pushing aside magazines and year books, I held them up and knew damn well those babies weren't getting over these thighs. But I tried anyway.

Even laying down on the bed wasn't getting them on. Butter and oil probably wouldn't have done me much good either.

I'm not exactly sure how, maybe because I stopped breathing for a whole minute, I got the jeans on. Only then I had to get up.

Another story all together.

I'm telling you right now, this was the shit funniest home videos were made of, I just knew it.

What was worse?

Me attempting to stand up with the tightest jeans on that I'd somehow managed to get myself into. All I needed was Jared to walk in on me at any moment during this state of extreme duress I was under. I wouldn't have been able to tell him not to come in if he knocked because breathing was optional. If I breathed I was sure the button would have flown off and broke the window.

When I did shimmy my way to a standing position, then I had to actually walk by bending my knees. I should have taken them off but I needed confirmation on this look though so I decided to face my fears. With a good amount of effort, I did the zombie walk out to the living room to get Jared's opinion.

Worst. Mistake. Ever.

Jared eyed the jeans, his smile nearly making his eyes squint closed as he held in what I knew was going to be the biggest fucking belly laugh known to man. "What are those, spandex or jeans?"

"My old jeans from high school." It hurt to speak because speaking required breathing and I only got to pick one.

"Why do you still have jeans from your senior year in high school?"

"I don't know. Why do you have old porn from college in your closet?"

He leveled me a serious look. "You can't just throw *porn out*. It never ages or deteriorates… or gets too big to fit… in jeans."

"Fuck you, Jared." I tried to relax my posture but the button was trying to poke a hole in my belly button. "Seriously, how do these look?"

I must have looked uncomfortable. Hell, I was uncomfortable. It was like someone was squeezing my gut like an anaconda squeezes the last breath out of its prey.

"Tallan, I hate to be honest but as your friend, and a guy, *and* someone who feels as much pain seeing you wear those jeans as you are obviously in … those are *way* too tight. Can you even breathe?"

"No," I gasped as I unzipped them feeling a little lightheaded due to lack of oxygen yet mostly relieved. "I can't breathe."

When I unzipped them I felt a little relief. But it wasn't enough. I had to get them off all the way. The problem was, they weren't coming off without assistance at that point. I got them on, just barely but getting them off was damn near impossible.

Jared must have sensed the panic because he looked over at me and set his beer on the end table. "What's wrong?"

"I can't get them off."

"You got them on… "

"Doesn't matter." I shook my head, nearing tears. How fucking embarrassing. "You should call 911. They're not coming off."

I'm claustrophobic. And these jeans were making me feel like I was enclosed in a tomb of denim. The shit was getting real and I wasn't discounting hyperventilating at this point. So when they wouldn't come off after five minutes of my frantic tugging, Jared began to laugh.

14

I'd lost all sense of stability and reached for the scissors in the drawer.

That's when Jared panicked. "Whoa!" He held up his hands in a calming manner, his palms raised as if he was going to try negotiating with me. "Put the scissors down."

"I can't take it any longer!" I held them up in the air. "I'm doing it!"

He stood from his place on the couch. "Here, let me do it then. You'll cut your leg off with as spastic as you are right now." And then he motioned for the couch. "Try it this way. You sit on the couch and I'll pull."

"I can't sit."

"Well, okay," he reached for the waistband and smiled, his chest pressed against mine. "You know, this isn't the first time I've taken your pants off." He teased, trying to lighten the situation.

"Jared?"

"Yes."

"I'm still holding the scissors."

"Got it." He pulled once more, tugged and pushed. They weren't budging. I was sure they were permanently a part of me. They had somehow merged with the epidermis of my skin to create this exoskeleton that would somehow protect me from future cellulite because, let's face it, I couldn't breathe wearing these jeans so eating was completely out of the question. I would forever be wearing Big Star jeans that were three sizes too small.

Jared stood once more, sweating and pushing his hair from his sticky forehead. "Okay, maybe we should cut them off."

I sighed. "Finally some reasoning."

Jared was hesitant with the scissors. Rightfully so, I guess. He was cutting jeans off someone. I'm not sure how it happens so quick in the ER when they cut clothing away but I guarantee you it's not slicing and dicing jeans as tight as these were. He could barely get the scissors between the fabric and my skin.

It took Jared ten minutes before they were off because he acted as if he was a blind man threading a needle.

Standing, he smiled when the fabric fell away and finally I could breathe. "And now your pants are off."

"Thank you." I sighed, because finally I could inhale and exhale and then grabbed at my stomach. "Jesus. That hurt."

"Should I do your shirt too? It looks tight." He squeezed the scissors in his hand.

Rolling my eyes, I smacked him with my elbow as I walked back to my room.

"Nice panties!" He yelled after me, laughing.

Chapter Two
BOXERS HANDSHAKE

Touching knuckles is how boxers greet each other whether they're wearing gloves or not. Touching gloves before the opening bell is also part of boxing protocol.

Tuesday
April 5, 2011

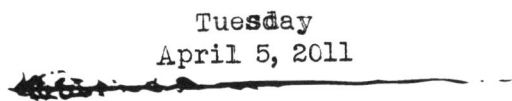

Everyone's heard that story about the small town boy moving on to bigger things. They've heard it because it's *so* common.

What you don't hear about it is what they left behind, and who was left oftentimes with a broken heart as the only remembrance that they were ever really there. Silas left *me* behind. And I never heard from him again. Until last night.

I knew why he left. I get it. He wanted to follow his dreams and he had the talent to do so. What I couldn't understand, and what I wanted to know was why couldn't he have those dreams that included me too?

Did I mean anything to him?

Four years together and then one day out of the blue and just days after high school graduation, as we made summer plans, he just up and left me.

He didn't even tell me in person. He called when he was in New York three days after graduation.

What did he say?

"I'm staying in New York. Sam thinks he can get me a record deal so I have to see what it could turn into."

Some four months later his music was being played on the radio. I never doubted for a minute that he could be a success. But was I so disposable that we couldn't have chased his dreams together?

I was the one left behind. And I do say left behind because life has literally left me behind since then.

I graduated last spring from Western Washington University. Since then I've been working as a freelance writer for blogs, magazines, newspapers, just where ever the money was. It paid the bills at least and allowed me the freedom of not having to go to a nine-to-five job.

The problem was I had to answer to those particular blogs, magazine, newspapers and no story was off limits. You want a story about ice fishing in the Antarctic; jock itch in Zimbabwe; or shearing sheep in Sweden and I got to write about it. Whoever wanted the story. Every time it was someone different too. Like right now. I'm working on an article for the *Seattle Times* on the Seattle Light Rail project. I can't say it's keeping my interest though and it doesn't help either that the editor involved is a total asshole.

Lauren Mitchel is a complete bitch and picks apart everything, and everyone. She's also the type of woman who gives you a deadline and then proceeds to send you reminders for a week about your upcoming due date. When you don't reply, she calls you.

"I need your article by two."

"Seriously?"

"Yes. Why would I joke about that?"

"I didn't know it was due today." I'm joking with her but she has no sense of humor. At all.

"Well, it is." Her tone was clipped. "Didn't you get my reminders I sent out?"

"Oh, well maybe."

"Awesome."

"Cool down, Lauren." Scrolling down in the document I checked the word count. "I'll have it to you soon."

"By two?"

"By one."

I managed to get the article to her by noon and wanted to tell her to un-bunch her panties because my shit was handled. I knew there'd be a ton of changes coming my way later but it always felt good to meet deadlines.

Thinking of deadlines got me thinking about Silas and my goal. I'd skipped lunch but by the time five rolled around I was starving. I don't know how people go without eating. I was certain that I would need assistance in losing the weight because the starvation diet wasn't going to cut it. The dreaded exercise word was floating around in my brain, trying to get pushed aside by the hungry neurons that were jumping ahead of it telling me to eat whatever I wanted. I was going to need a professional.

The thought of going to a gym was about as appealing as starving myself. I didn't want people staring and judging me when I worked out. I didn't want to sweat in public. I didn't want to sit on places where people had left sweat outlines of their ass. I didn't want to be tortured by the clock as each interminable minute ticked by while doing said sweating.

In college I wrote a paper for the school newspaper regarding the gym equipment and how sanitary those machines were. There'd been a recent flu epidemic at the school and students were blaming the gym. That had me in the gym every day for a week doing research.

It was awful the way the boys stared at the women when they worked out. Like they were there just for that purpose. And let me tell you, some of the girls were just as bad. Maybe it was because we were in college and sex is constantly on the mind, but still, I didn't want an experience like that when I was attempting to lose weight. And did I mention the sweat and the germs that make permanent homes in the gym only to relocate to a newer address…specifically on you?

My phone buzzed with a missed call from Jared. More than likely he was wondering where I was. Usually I worked from our apartment but our internet service had been sketchy lately so I worked at Starbucks today. And avoided mochas all day. If that wasn't the true test of my determination to get my ass back in shape, nothing was.

Jared and I have been doing Taco Tuesday for years. It's our thing since freshman year in college and continued well past the freshmen fifteen that I'd accumulated. Now we live together so it's kind of a must.

It's never been romantic between us. We have always been just friends. We did try the romantic part though. Even had the most awkward sex ever our sophomore year. But still, even after that, we remained friends. He's great and always had my back no matter what. He's the one person I can trust to give me an honest answer. Like if your jeans are too tight. And I needed brutal honesty. Jared was the man. He will tell me shit that even I don't want to hear at times. I am thankful for it though. If it wasn't for him I would still be in those jeans right now.

My phone beeped again letting me know I had a message. Jared said he needed cilantro for the tacos so I walked up 1st Street to Safeway.

When I got back to our third floor apartment on Republic I was lightheaded from not eating. Jared was in the kitchen chopping cabbage. The smell of spiced chicken and chili powder hit me as soon as I opened the door. I almost collapsed at his feet in prayer thanking him for the smells assaulting my food deprived nostrils.

Jared had an amazing recipe handed down from his mother who was Mexican. The best part wasn't even the meat. For me, I'm a carb girl. I love it. Bread, flour, pastries, anything made from wheat or corn. So what completed the tacos for me was the corn tortillas he made from scratch in a cast iron pan. Then to top them off, he sprinkled them with Johnny's Seasoning salt. They were to die for. When we were in college he made them for me for the first time and if there would have been any sort of chemistry between us, I would have married him based on his ability to make taco shells like that. Any man who could cook in my opinion was worth putting a ring on it.

"Welcome home, honey!"

Jared Stevens would be the perfect guy for some girl, some day. He had some commitment phobia but he was hot. He wasn't always such a looker. In college he was kinda awkward but I think a lot of us were. It was some time after junior year when he started to resemble a man and began to fill out in places that makes girls stupid. And he was about to be a man in uniform so watch out ladies.

Having just graduated from the police academy, he was every woman's dream in a uniform. Now he was starting his four weeks in field training learning the laws and patrolling Seattle before he started his one year probation with the precinct.

He wasn't in uniform now, instead he was in an old ratty black t-shirt and basketball shorts, usually what he wore at home. When I walked into the kitchen, he smiled and pushed the bowl of salsa in my direction.

Half Mexican, his skin is nice and tan, rare blue eyes, dark hair and that body caused the angels to sing when he bared the goods. I had a feeling Jared wouldn't be single for long. Occasionally he had girls over, but not often. I rarely saw them more than once, twice if they made a lot of noise. The walk of shame they did was often more shameful for me when I'd run into them on the way to the bathroom the morning after knowing how pathetic they were and that they probably wouldn't be walking these hallowed halls again. Jared was a looker but he was in no way a keeper of those girls' hearts.

"Smells delicious." Looking around the kitchen I remembered the parts of Taco Tuesday I hated. This part is why Jared is single. I'm sure of it. He never cleans up after himself and makes a complete mess when he cooks. I guess we can't have our cake and eat it too. Ahhhh, cake, now there's something I could go for right about now, right after these delicious tacos I'm about to inhale.

Taking the trash can in hand, I attempted to clean up the vegetables he didn't use and the bags he had scattered around.

"Did you make that peach pie?" He asked, his eyes focused on the chopping.

"Yeah," I motioned toward the fridge. "It's in there." Reaching over him I grabbed what looked to be garlic.

"I'm not done with that."

Did I mention Jared makes his own salsa, too?

It doesn't lend well for clean-up, but it's so good you forget that part. It's sweet with a kick of garlic and cilantro and so fucking delicious you could just eat that for dinner. I have before. Throw that shit together with some corn chips and it's a little slice of heaven straight from Mexico.

The chips were on the counter in a bright blue bowl so I dug in immediately taking much larger scoops than necessary. All the while, salsa was dribbling down my chin and onto my shirt.

Damn it, that shit always happens.

And this is why I'm single and trying to lose weight with salsa stains on my shirt and trying to fit in jeans that should have been retired after my freshman year of college

"How was patrolling today?" I asked with a mouthful of chips spitting tiny pieces onto the counter.

Yet another reason why I'm single.

"Good." He nodded laughing at my impeccable lady-like manners. Reaching inside the bag, Jared took the cilantro, washed it, and then began chopping it. He added that to the salsa, stirred it with his finger, and then placed the rest in the bowl next to the chips to add to our tacos. I'd marry him if we weren't the bestest of friends.

I was jealous of Jared's cooking abilities. I could bake but when it came to actually presenting a meal, couldn't do it.

"It's almost ready. Grab some plates and beer?"

Nodding, I took one more bite of salsa and then retrieved our plates and cerveza. Jared put a lime in each Corona as we sat down at the table. I took another lime and squeezed it over my tacos. As I sat there looking at my heaping plate of three tacos, and then the beer, I began to wonder if this was a good idea. I knew it wasn't but still, who could pass these up?

It's like in order to lose weight you have to stop living. I bet skinny people are depressed. I hear them say they have more energy when they exercise but I think that might just be their brain's way of fooling them into thinking they're happy.

After the third taco, I looked down at my plate in sadness. "Ugh! Damn you, delicious bastards!" I pushed aside the last taco but it felt so wrong to let it go to waste. What if I started dieting tomorrow? Or maybe just made them healthier? "I bet if you didn't fry the shells I could still eat them."

Jared looked at me as if I just said I hated them. "You can't mess with the recipe, Tallan. Maybe if you didn't put a pound of cheese on each taco."

"Don't be rude." And then I said probably the least truthful statement of the evening. "You could stand to lose a pound too, donut boy."

"Oh, bullshit." Jared stood knocking the table a little and lifted his shirt.

I was wrong. As I eyed his washboard stomach I felt even worse about eating the tacos. "Fuck you and those rock hard abs of absolute heaven you have. Don't mind me as I walk away wiggling and jiggling in shame like a bowl full of Jell-O."

"That's what I thought." He sat back down and started in on his fifth taco. It has to be the muscles that eat up all the extra calories that men can consume. Jerks. One more cross to bear for women. Life is sooooo not fair.

"You don't need to do this." His voice was suddenly tender. "You're not eighteen anymore and you look fine."

"Ordinarily I wouldn't, but, Silas was the love of my life. You know that. And to have a chance to see him again," I shrugged. "I just want to prove to him I still look good."

"And you do. So what's the problem?"

"I don't look like I did in high school."

"And you shouldn't." Jared set his taco down and gave me a serious look, his eyebrows raised in question. "You're twenty-two. There's a difference between eighteen and twenty-two."

"Yeah, like twenty pounds."

"So you're meeting him to show him you lost weight? Why don't you just snap chat him or something."

"It's not just that. I want answers. He left me with no explanation as to why we couldn't do this thing together and I want to face him in person. I want him to regret leaving me before he ravages my body backstage for all the world to see."

Jared shook his head now. The more I talked the worse it got. "And you can't get answers over the phone?"

"No."

"So what," he relaxed and leaned back in the chair crossing his arms over his chest. He was going into protective mode. "You're going to talk to him and then fuck him?"

Rolling my eyes I picked my plate up and set it on the counter, and then looked out the kitchen window at the street below. "Don't be an ass."

"Hey, I'm just trying to understand. He can get pussy anywhere he wants. Why you?"

"Way to make me feel completely inadequate, Jared."

"I never said you were inadequate. What I asked was why he would call his old girlfriend for pussy. He's in town for one night. How do you think it's going to end?"

He had a very good point. I knew what Silas wanted but who was Jared to judge me? So what if he wanted one night? What if he wanted more than one? Was I fooling myself to think there would be anything more than one night?

Probably.

Mostly I wanted answers from Silas and for that I would meet him in six weeks. And you know what, excuse the fuck out of me for wanting some rock dick. Even back in high school Silas was amazing in bed. Nothing compared to the nights we shared together and I wanted that again.

"I just want to lose twenty pounds." I finally said to Jared as we did dishes. "What do you do to get into shape?"

"I masturbate."

"Jared... " Shaking my head I handed him the cast iron pan for him to clean. "I'm serious."

He shrugged. "So am I."

He probably was knowing him.

"Just go to the gym."

I groaned at the thought. "I don't want to go to a gym. Everyone

24

will stare at me."

"Why?"

He clearly had never had an experience like I did. But look at him. Of course he didn't.

"Men at the gym are all judgy and staring. The women are so fucking skinny they look like little boys. I bet my ankles are bigger than most of their calves. And the women just compare each other... who has the bigger ass, who has the most cellulite, who isn't spinning or running fast enough. It's disgusting."

"You're exaggerating." Jared looked down at my ankles, his eyes widened.

I punched his shoulder. "Don't be mean."

"You're the one who pointed your freakishly large ankles out. My God, Tallan. Can you even find ankle socks to fit over those? I think I've heard those things called 'cankles' by others who aren't as ankle-endowed as you seem to be."

"Shut. Up." I stalked toward the fridge. "How about that pie? I'll start tomorrow."

I laid in bed that night, after eating two slices of pie, and I couldn't sleep thinking about my goal and an article I had to get done for a blog that was due tomorrow. That's when I decided to get up and look to see what else was in that box I kept from high school.

My yearbooks. It was filled with memories and photos of me and Silas. There wasn't a moment from the time I met him, until the day he left that I didn't think we would be together always. Everyone thought we would be. Nothing could have prepared me for him leaving but then again, I think there was a small part of me that had prepared myself for this possibility. A man with his talent wasn't going to stay in Seattle forever. At least not without leaving first.

Maybe that's why he was coming back. Maybe he wanted to finally settle down?

I'll admit my thought gave me more hope than it should have. Expecting a rock star of his status to want to settle down was stupid of me, but the thought was there regardless.

That sort of thing happened in real life, right?

Turning the page in the book, my eyes landed on the one of Silas and me at Homecoming our senior year. We looked happy and in love. The next series of photos beside it was ones of him on stage rocking out with his band. It was that night when I knew he would make it big someday. He had to. Little did I know I wouldn't be a part of that. The idea that maybe he might still want me gave my heart that familiar flutter of excitement. So if I wanted some closure, or possibly some way to reconnect and reignite this old flame, then who had the right to judge or take that opportunity away from me? I didn't have a voice in him leaving but you can bet your jiggly ass I was going to have a voice in him wanting more from me than just one night.

Wednesday
April 6, 2011

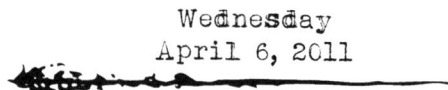

The next morning I was trying to decide what to eat for breakfast and basically just standing in the kitchen staring at the fridge. I couldn't find a damn thing worth eating so I toasted a slice of bread and put butter on it while I waited for the coffee to finish.

Jared came into the kitchen dressed in his uniform ready for work. "Give me that. You're dieting, cankle queen."

I glared and he laughed eating my toast. He stopped and held the toast between his lips, his palms raised. "You know damn well I find you attractive and I'm joking with you."

"You find me attractive?"

"You know I do. We've had sex before and I came within what, a minute? Remember?"

"That was different. We were drunk and that was in college. Shit's changed since then."

"How so?"

"Well, we don't have sex and we're not attracted to each other like that."

Jared nodded finishing off the toast and then stealing my cup of coffee too. "Let's clear that up. You're my friend. Probably my best friend these days since Jay got married. And you're hot whether you want to see it or not. Yeah, we don't have sex. But that's only because you said when we moved in together that we couldn't." He laughed, his voice turning playful. "Which seems stupid to me. I think we should be able to relieve stress sometimes without the awkwardness of the morning walk of shame."

Jared knew why we couldn't have sex. I thought of him as my big brother, though I was older than him by two weeks. I just didn't find him attractive in that way.

"What's your point?"

"My point is… I find you attractive. Even though we will always be friends, that's not to say I don't think of you naked sometimes."

"Friends?"

He looked panicked. "Yes… where exactly did you think I was going with that?"

"That you were going to tell me you've always secretly loved me and want to get married?"

"You totally missed my point then. But yes, I do love you in a sisterly way. You're far too annoying for wife material." And then he eyed my ankles. "And if we had babies they would have your ankles. That's definitely the dominant gene in that equation. Poor kids."

"I pity the woman who you finally do marry. I'm not sure there will be room in the marriage for the two of you."

Jared turned and started to walk out the door but slapped my ass. "I could say the same to you."

"Dick."

I was halfway through my article for the blog when Jared came home early.

"You remember Danny, right?"

I made sure to save the document I was working on. "That bar owner you're always checking on?"

"Yeah, him."

"So?" I turned in my chair to face him.

"Well, he has a nephew who's apparently a bad ass at training."

"To do what, drink?"

"No, dumb ass. Getting in shape. And you wouldn't have to go to a gym."

"Okay… " I took a deep breath trying to prepare myself. "Who?"

"Destry Stone." He seemed so proud of himself but it took me a minute to understand, or remember who Destry was. The name sounded so familiar.

"The boxer?"

"Yeah!"

This was like the best news ever. He could totally get me in shape. It'd be like boot camp but with a heavyweight boxer. I wondered if I'd get abs like Jared's…or a boxer's…in six weeks?

Jared wrote down the number on my note pad and then went back to work. I called it right away to arrange a time. The number was for the bar so I set up a time with Danny, the owner, and he said he'd pass the information along to Destry.

If I could get this shit accomplished in less than six weeks, I could go back to eating what I wanted. Surely a boxer could whip my ass in shape in less than forty-two days, right? My stomach and those high school jeans that died an untimely death were banking on that.

Bring it on.

Chapter Three
CHIN

Having a chin, whiskers or granite like jaw means having the ability to absorb punches when you get hit with a big shot and stay standing, to remain on your feet despite seeing black flashing lights, blurred, double or triple vision and feeling a buzz that goes all the way to your toes. Some say you are either born with a good chin or not. Others say it's a mental toughness that when your brain tells you to go down to the canvas you will yourself to stay on your feet.

Thursday
April 7, 2011

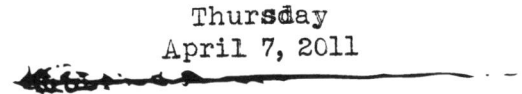

The next morning I was sitting at my computer working.

Lie. I was Googling Silas Cade.

What I found out was his string of women he'd been spotted with between strippers, actresses, models, you name it, he'd been with them. He was now covered in tattoos, had a few piercings, rumored to have his dick pierced and what some would say an unsustainable sex drive.

And then I started in with images and trying to find the best one I could of him. I went through his Twitter and Instagram pages, all filled with him in exotic places in a variety of poses with beautiful women.

Eventually I found one of him and a beautiful woman that was perfect for cropping. I cropped her out of the photo and placed myself beside him to see if I even looked good anymore next to him. And after just a moment of dissecting everything I hated about my body, I realized I looked like hell next to him. Not even comparable. I looked like I ate part of him for breakfast or that I could have been his mom with the way I hovered over him.

"My precious." I grumbled in the best Gollum voice from the *Lord of the Rings'* movies that I could muster all the while petting the screen.

That's when I realized I could resize the photo on the screen and minimize myself to a more natural height. There's also this feature that makes you look skinnier.

So I sized myself down a bit more, looked like a stack of bones but I still didn't look right next to him. He was perfection with his jet black hair, brown pleading eyes and marked skin.

"Wow, you really trimmed down." Jared said, resting his chin on my shoulder. I hadn't even heard him come home.

I reached up with my fist and punched his throat. "You're on duty, asshole. Why do you keep showing up here in the middle of the day?"

He coughed grabbing at his throat. "I left my phone here."

"Do you do anything at work? How do you have time to just stop by your apartment?"

"Part of my job is patrolling. All of my job is patrolling." Creating a few feet of distance between us he looked back at the door. "Why was the door unlocked? We've talked about this. When I'm not here it needs to stay locked."

"Because I forgot to lock it."

"Yes, clearly you were preoccupied." He motioned to the screen with a half-smile and walked into the kitchen. "Seriously though, Tallan. Lock it. There's assholes out there."

I rolled my eyes and closed the Photoshop program. "Whatever, Jared."

"Don't whatever me. You won't be saying whatever when a guy shows up to rob us, sees you're here and kills you *after* he rapes you for being in the wrong place at the wrong time."

"You're right." I smiled. "I won't be saying that. Because I would be dead."

I followed him out of the kitchen when he found his phone. He held it up when he got to the door leaning against the frame. "Just lock the door."

"Fine. I will." Taking the hair-tie from my wrist I put my hair up in a ponytail.

Jared gave me a funny look and I knew where that was going. "Why did you do that to the photo?"

"Do what?"

"Make yourself look like that. I thought we talked about that last night?"

"Go. To. Work."

"Fine." He sighed reaching for the door knob. "I'm going."

"When do you get off tonight?"

"Probably when Catie comes over later." He said suggestively, winking.

"Gross. Stop sleeping with my friends. It's weird."

Jared stepped out the door and smiled, twisting around to walk backwards down the hall. "Just keeping the city happy."

"I'm sure."

When he got to the end of the hall, he yelled over his shoulder. "Lock it up!"

It wasn't ten minutes after Jared left, maybe ten minutes, and my phone rang. It was the call I was waiting for.

"Tallan?"

"Yep."

There was a slight pause before he cleared his throat. "It's Destry. My Uncle Danny said you were looking for a personal trainer?"

"Yeah, yes, I am." I was stuttering through my words.

"Okay…" I could hear what sounded like music and commotion in the background, and then a door slamming closed.

"Do you work out at a gym I could meet you at?"

Please say no.

Jared had said the session would either be at our house or his house but I didn't want to assume anything.

"No. We can do it at my Uncle's bar. There's a basement."

A basement? I could do a basement for sure. Low lighting, probably no mirrors. Even better.

"Come by the bar around six?"

My eyes went wide and I nearly dropped the phone. "Today?"

"Yes."

I started to panic just a little. Tonight was so sudden. I had to mentally prepare for these types of things. It took me weeks to mentally prepare myself to call and make a gynecology appointment. And then the appointment had to be set for at least three weeks after the call so I could do some more mental acrobatics. Tonight to start training was throwing me in a tailspin.

"Okay, see you then." I finally said when I realized he was waiting for a reply.

"Yep." And then he hung up. That was it.

I spent the rest of the afternoon looking through my closet for something to wear that wouldn't make me look huge. I ended up going for black yoga pants, though I hadn't done yoga a day in my life and a loose fitting t-shirt. Around five I headed over to Alaskan Way. The cab driver dropped me at Pier 57 so all I had to do was cross the street over to Danny's Bar.

That's when I got nervous to the point I thought I was going to vomit. I've been to the gym before. No way did I want that guy who banged the weights around and grunted like he was fucking someone with each chest press. Or the ones who flex in the mirror and spend more time checking themselves and the women out.

I knew this experience was going to be completely different but I wasn't sure how. Could be bad, could be good.

You're doing this for just six weeks. You can do it.

Once inside the doors, the bar was smoky and smelled like someone pissed outside the door. Thank God I carried hand sanitizer. The smell alone made me gasp. Urine and smoke just isn't a good combination.

To the left of the door were four pool tables, to the right, about ten cocktail tables surrounded by flat screen televisions. In the middle of the room was the bar, black wood surrounded by old metal chairs. On the back wall was a floor-to-ceiling mirror with glass shelves that housed the liquor.

"Can I get you a drink?" I looked up, my eyes drawn to the man before me. He was standing behind the bar, arms crossed over his chest, green tired eyes met mine that seemed too dull for this time of day. It's not from the dim lighting that his eyes looked that dull either. It's clear he's lived beyond his years. A thick golden beard hid the lines on his face. "Drink?" he asked again.

"No, I'm meeting someone."

"They all are, sweetie." He cracked a smile but then turned toward the man next to him. "Good to see you, Larry. What'll it be?"

"Blue Moon." The man said spilling immediately into conversation about the baseball game on the TV behind the bar.

Though the voices around me kept grabbing my attention, I couldn't focus on any one in particular.

I kept going over what I was going to say to Destry and why I was doing this in the first place. Here I was about to meet a heavyweight champion boxer. Well, former heavyweight. He'd lost his title this past winter to a boxer from Canada, Ray Lucas.

Just the thought of meeting Destry was nerve wracking. Imagine how I'll be at the concert and seeing Silas again.

"Are you Tallan Spencer?" Someone asked from behind me. I spun around on the stool to face the voice.

Holy. Shit. Look at him.

Wearing a dark gray t-shirt and black shorts was probably the hottest man I've ever seen. I'm not kidding you. He's even better looking than Silas and Jared combined.

This guy was the one you had your fantasies about. And they would be just that, a fantasy because men like this just don't exist in real life.

Only he did. He was tall, perfect tanned skin and muscles that seemed to bulge in all the right places.

A pair of bright green eyes drifted my way, or maybe I drifted their way. I wanted to walk away right then. No way was I sweating around this guy. Extreme amounts of self-consciousness set in right then. I even stood up a little straighter.

With a nod toward the back of the bar, he took me down a dark staircase with black walls and concrete steps. We went down what seemed like forever and then through another door. He motioned to the right. "That's the bathroom."

Nothing in this bar screamed sanitary. There was absolutely no way I was ever using that bathroom. No fucking way.

I understood the smell outside. I would gladly relieve myself on a crowded street during Mardi Gras before I'd step foot in that bathroom right there.

I laughed, trying to make light of the room. There was no equipment that I could see. Just a boxing ring in the center of the room.

"Is this like a fight club down here. Is the first rule we don't talk about it?"

He didn't even look back at me when he spoke, instead he turned away even more so and turned on a series of lights. "I'm not here to make jokes."

Okay. So no sense of humor at all. Got it.

"They said you were looking for a personal trainer, yes?"

"Yes." Shaking my head I tried to get myself to focus around him. "I am."

Leaning against the wall his arms crossed over his chest. My eyes immediately went to his forearms and how it was possible to have so many different muscles in your arms. I never even knew there were that many. "What are your goals here?"

I swallowed trying to focus. "My goals?"

"Yeah, what the hell do you want to accomplish? You want to lose weight? Want to wear the matching outfits, what? Danny said you needed to lose weight but I'm not seeing it."

"Yes. Twenty pounds and I have a very tight six week deadline."

"That's not exactly healthy to lose that much weight in that short of time. Why six weeks?"

"Because I'm meeting a friend and I don't want him to see me like this."

"And 'like this' you mean what?"

Jesus. Was he really wanting me to say it? To voice that image that almost every woman in America has?

"Fat… "

"So you're doing this for someone else, not for your desire to get healthy on your own?"

"Well, yeah… "

His face was blank as he spoke, no emotion at all. "Why?"

"Why what?"

His brow scrunched in confusion. "Why do this for someone else."

"I don't know. I just don't want him to see me out of shape. I used to have this tight body in high school and then… well, now I look like this."

"This isn't yoga, you know that right?"

I nodded, not sure how else to respond.

"I'll have you screaming for me to let up."

Oh God, why was I thinking something dirty right now?

He gave me this once over, as if he was judging me and deciding on a plan. Or checking me out. Could have been either one at that point. Regardless, I was nothing short of uncomfortable. Being scrutinized like this, by someone who so obviously lived and breathed inside of a gym at least four hours a day, every day, made this once over even worse.

"What do you do for exercise now?"

"Stairs?"

"That shouldn't be a question." He noted, barely making eye contact with me.

"Well, it's not exactly exercise but I walk up three flights of stairs every day."

"That's all? Just stairs? And you think you can hang with the likes of me training you?"

What was he expecting me to say?

"Yes. I heard you were the best and I need the best to keep me motivated."

"I'm not your fucking cheering squad or your pep rally, you either want this or you don't."

I felt completely ridiculous around him. Like I wanted to cover myself up and never let him see an ounce of my skin in fear he'd be so disgusted with my slightly overweight body compared to his physique.

I bet that's why his last name is Stone. He's carved from stone, like the fucking David statue, oh my God, I wonder if he's truly sporting all of David's stone-like features? Focus, Tallan, focus and don't let your mind go there…like *ever!*

"What about your diet?"

"Uh… "

"To me diet isn't nearly as important as exercise. You need to get your heart rate up every day. Most disagree and think you can just control your weight by dieting but I'm a firm believer in exercise and cardio."

"So, like running?"

"Not necessarily. Cardio. That can be anything that gets your heart rate up every day for a set amount of time. The longer your heart rate is up, the more calories you burn, your muscles become more efficient, it's all tied together."

Immediately, and I do mean immediately, with the look on his face I was thinking about sex and that damn David statue again and being tied together. I couldn't help it. He was talking about getting your heart rate up…among other things…and, well, look at him. Anyone in their right mind had those thoughts about this man and him getting my heart rate up had me jumping right into bed with him. I'm not in my right mind. Well, at least I wasn't right then.

I bet he was good in bed. I bet he was fantastic even. All sweaty and muscular. He shifted his stance right then to scratch his head and I got a little sneaky peek at his abs.

Oh yeah, he's good in bed. You can't be ripped like that when abdominals were formed as perfectly as his were and moved like they did and not be amazing in bed. It was a given.

Looking around, I tried to focus on anything but him. I had to. That's when I noticed there was no gym equipment around.

"What do you work out with?"

"I'm not the one working out. You are. And you don't need all that fancy shit. Just stick to the basics. Add some weights and you'll be good."

"Okay, so what's basics?"

"I told you, cardio. And then you'll do lunges, squats, pushups, sit-ups." He gave me a look, one that knew I was overwhelmed easily by his presence. "We'll start with some upper body and then tomorrow we'll work on the lower body. Alternate a different group of muscles."

Everything he was saying wasn't making much sense but judging by his body, he knew damn well what he was doing.

He gave me a nod toward the wall. "Start with some upper body. Choose a set of dumbbells and I want you to do ten reps each. Three sets per exercise."

"Okay…"

"You're going to do a hammer curl, tricep kick back, incline curl, overhead tricep extension with your palms down, overhead curl, and then an overhead tricep extension with your palms forward."

He was speaking Greek. Was David Greek? Oh damn, I gotta get focused.

Destry must have known I had no idea what he was talking about. Rolling his eyes he proceeded to demonstrate each exercise with the free weights. "Hammer curl…" With his hands hanging loosely at his sides, he widened his stance and straightened out his body. With the weights pointed vertical, he lifted the weights so his forearms curled up against his biceps.

After that he leaned one knee on the bench, placed his left palm flat against the leather padded seat and then took his right arm and extended it back coming in line with his side. "Tricep kick back."

Adjusting the bench, he seated it at an angle, sat down with his back pressed against the bench and curled his arms up. "Inclined curl." Sitting up again, he took the weights over his head, let them fall back so his elbows were bent and then straightened them out over his head. "Overhead tricep extension with your palms forward."

I'm not sure I followed all that but it was fun to watch.

"Are you going to just stare at me or are you serious about this? If you aren't serious then stop wasting my fucking time and your money."

I was speechless, like really at a loss for words. Of course I was serious, I was here putting up with this humiliation wasn't I?

"I'm trying to understand all the terminology...did I mention that my go-to form of exercise is walking up stairs?" I tried to hide my smile when I noticed he wanted to grin as well but instead it showed itself as a condescending smirk.

"Just don't waste my time, I'm not helping you for my own entertainment, I've got more important things I could be doing."

Alrighty then.

"So why lifting weights?" I was trying to lighten the mood seeing that he acted as if this was a total waste of his time.

He set the dumbbell on the concrete floor and stood up straight, his hands on his hips. "By increasing your muscle mass you will increase your metabolism meaning you'll burn more calories."

My eyes were probably a little wide but he never said anything about it. Hell, he wasn't even looking at me. "Get started, you've got five minutes."

And then he disappeared.

In front of me on the brick wall was a mirror covered in dust so I wiped that down with my towel and then grabbed a set of weights. The ones he gave me were way too heavy so I reached for the lighter ones. I can honestly say right now was the first time I had ever lifted weights to exercise. That seems pathetic but in high school my weight was never a problem. In college I took the whole "Freshman Fifteen" to another level. If it didn't involve beer or pizza or beer, I wasn't part of it. Hence why I'm here right now.

As I stood in front of the mirror I looked at my form. I had no form. My body was slightly hunched forward like a newborn baby afraid to sprawl out. Standing a little straighter I let my arms hang down with the weights and watched myself do the hammer curl Destry showed me.

It wasn't so bad, it was worse, and before I knew it I had done three sets like he said. And five minutes later he returned and had me do them all over again while he watched…and judged…and scrutinized…*and never said a word.* I want to scream at him, in frustration, say something, asshole, just don't sit there and stare at me as I die a slow death.

My pathetic excuse for arms and the non-existent muscles inside were screaming in anger at me. If my arms hurt this bad after doing ten minutes of only working out my arms, how in the hell was I going to be able to get through six weeks of this?

"How much more of this do I have to do?" I asked with irritation, about ten seconds away from crying. I think he knew it too. But it did nothing to stop him from ordering more.

"You're not done." He said, making me do another set.

He was trying to kill me. I was sure of it.

There I was glaring at him, wishing a slow, painful death for him and he was acting like I wasn't even there as he stared at a magazine in front of him with his legs kicked up on a metal chair.

"This is ridiculous!" I shouted after another set of those stupid hammer curls. I wanted to shove the weight up his ass at that point. Right on up there.

My words earned me a glare, those bright green eyes didn't look so bright with the scowl on that gorgeous face. "Did I mention that if you're not serious, don't waste my fucking time?"

I grumbled to myself but continued.

And the pain continued, in fact, another forty-five minutes of pain until the Muscle Warden released me from this muscle-filled prison of torture.

When I left that night around nine, I could barely lift my arms and I knew one thing for certain. I hated Destry Stone.

Chapter Four

DIRTY FIGHTING

Holding an opponent's head down and hitting their face with uppercuts or ribs with hooks, rabbit punches, elbowing, forearm in the throat, armbar in a clinch, late punches, low blows, step on an opponent's foot and punch, continuous headbutting and making it look accidental.

Friday
April 8, 2011

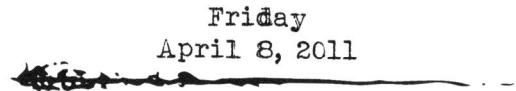

I'm dead. No, by the soreness in my upper body, I was most certainly alive. I *wanted* to be dead. Make. The. Pain. Stop.

Thankfully, I could *pretend* I was dead all day because I had nothing to work on Friday morning. And it was clearly a good thing because there was no way I could type. No way my fingers were working. The pain even extended to my fingernails. How the hell does a person's fingernails hurt?

Breathing hurt. I tried to stop breathing. Didn't work. Even no movement hurt.

Eventually I tried to roll over. That was so much worse. I had to go pee. Or I could pee in the bed. Who would really judge me at this point? There comes a time in one's life where peeing on yourself is acceptable. Sure, that was typically past the age of seventy that this was allowed but clearly the pain I was in warranted a few decades of forgiveness.

After much consideration, I realized that I would have to wash my sheets and I didn't have the stamina or the energy to go pee so washing urine filled laundry wasn't happening either.

"Jared!" I screamed trying to find someone to help me. Maybe he could bring me something to pee in or at least help me to the bathroom.

Unfortunately for me, he didn't answer. When I looked at the clock it was already ten that morning. He was at work.

Fuck.

I was on my own. Or I could call Catie.

Yes, excellent plan.

I texted her, the motion to actually retrieve my phone wasn't easy and neither was using my fingers. When the text went through, I heard the beep coming from Jared's room. Figures she stayed over. I hadn't even noticed her being here last night. But I also didn't notice much of anything. After the workout I went straight from the shower to my bed and never moved. Woke up in the same spot as I was when I hit the bed.

What? Catie texted back.

Come over here.

I uh, it may take me a while.

Why?

To get there.

Stop bullshitting. I heard your phone beep from the other room. If you're trying to hide your affair from me, turn your phone on silent.

She came over after that, all shameful and flushed that I caught her. I really didn't care if she slept with Jared. Made absolutely no difference to me. Pain was my only friend right now, and fuck if Catie wasn't going to meet my new bestie since she was screwing my roommate.

"Why do you look like you're hung over?" Catie sat down on my bed, assessing me as she put her long blonde hair up in a messy bun. She was dressed in one of Jared's flannel shirts with the buttons mismatched. I could see her boobs but modesty was never a trait Catie possessed.

I tried to sit up but then gave up and laid there longer, my heavy arms rested on my stomach. "I worked out last night."

"Have you ever worked out?"

"Nope." I yawned, even that hurt, and continued staring at the ceiling. "Which is why I look like this."

"I see."

I've known Catie for two years. We met in our journalism class and quickly became friends. She lived in Marysville, worked for the local paper but came into Seattle often to see Jared. I'm sure she came to see me too, but I couldn't blame her for choosing dick over me. I would if I was her.

"Wanna get breakfast?"

"No." I gave her a look of disgust. "I can't move. And I can't eat. I'm dieting."

"Why?"

"I'm meeting an old high school friend in six weeks." I motioned to myself, tried to at least. "I can't look like this."

"Like what? All curvy and beautiful?"

"No. Jelly like."

"Come on. Seriously. I'm hungry. Let's go to Urbane Café."

I loved Urbane Café and she knew it. She was taunting me. Baiting me with a carrot. Only the carrot was their delicious carb and starch-filled potatoes.

Just as I was considering going to the Urbane Café, I thought about Silas and my plan, then decided not to go. "I can't. I'll just eat eggs here."

"They have eggs there."

Of course she had to point that out. Catie was beginning to sell me on the idea and she knew it. Problem was, I couldn't actually move.

"If we go, you might have to actually carry me there. Do you have one of those strollers?"

"I could borrow my sister's. She just had a baby."

"They have weight limits on those things."

I raised an eyebrow at her. "Way to kick me when I'm down."

"What about a shopping cart?" Catie held back a smile. "That guy on the corner has one. Maybe he'd let us borrow it if we promise to bring him breakfast."

"Yeah, I could ask him. Food is always a big motivator for people who live out of shopping carts."

I held my arm up, well, as best as I could. "And before we go, I need you to carry me to the bathroom and help me to pee. I need to make room for those eggs and potatoes."

Catie had no idea what she was in for this morning.

I was able to get out of bed but it wasn't easy. Catie thought it was hilarious. Asshole.

"So who's responsible for this?" She asked when I sat down on the toilet. I didn't care one bit that she was watching me pee.

"Destry Stone." I growled when I stood, hunched over and walking like I was, well, sore. We walked into the living room where I contemplated changing out of my sweatpants but then decided that was too much work.

"Ohhhh… " Catie raised her eyebrows as she reached for her bag on the kitchen counter. "Tell me more."

"Later. Let's eat first. I don't want to think about him right now."

Catie had a car but it was easier to take the bus around Seattle. On the way there she asked about Silas. Everyone knew who Silas Cade was. But she probably didn't know I used to date him. Most people you told never believed you anyways. I mean, why would they believe you dated a rock star?

That's like saying you once fucked Brad Pitt. Never happened once they're famous unless you had a video to prove it.

I had a feeling Jared had told Catie because for one, Jared believed me, and two, I had pictures of us in high school.

When Catie asked about Silas, I went all giddy on her. "He's coming to town in six weeks and called the other night to have me meet up with him."

"Do you think he wants to get back together?"

I sighed, and it hurt to do so. "No, probably not but whatever happens, I'm going to make it a night he's *never* going to forget. That much I can do."

Catie smiled. "Good for you, girl. Rock that boy's night!"

"At least someone's happy for me. Jared's being all weird about it."

"He's just worried about you. It's in his nature. He's always been protective."

She got me thinking about Silas again, and a little nervous about the meeting. I did wonder what he wanted, how he'd react, all that. Would I be nervous? How much had he changed?

From pictures and articles—and the life he was leading—he had most certainly changed.

When we got to the restaurant, and seated at the bar with its white walls and clean glass surface, she asked about Destry again.

"So what's he like?" She asked while I drooled over her potatoes and bacon.

"He's a fucking asshole."

"Tell me how you *really* feel." Catie laughed, barely keeping her food in her mouth.

"Can't sugarcoat it. The guy is a tool. I know what his deal is but he's mean. Just plain mean."

"Hmmm," she paused, "that sucks. Too bad he's not nice. I mean, from what I've seen he's a total hottie."

"He's certainly hot. It's the personality that sucks."

"Maybe he's been fucked over too many times. I mean, he can't be that bad. He had a steady girlfriend for two years. You know how he lost the title, right?"

"Two years? That's surprising. And no, I didn't know that." I wasn't even sure I cared, but I asked anyways. "Why?" I'd been so busy Googling Silas these days I failed to do the proper research on the man I was paying $100 dollars a week to get me in shape. Not researching someone, or something, was rare for me. I did research on everything. Even bottled water.

"Well, some say he lost it because he wasn't trained enough and got into the ring unprepared. But then it's rumored he lost the fight on purpose."

"You mean like it was fixed?"

"Yeah… "

"Who said that?"

Catie shrugged. "Reporters, I guess."

"Fixing a fight is illegal. He would have been suspended, wouldn't he?"

"Probably. But no one could prove he lost on purpose, from what I've heard. And Destry denied it."

When Catie and I got back from breakfast, she left and I took a nap. I had to. Just going to breakfast had exhausted me. This getting in shape was no bullshit.

When I got up I went through my email and saw a few that needed attention.

One was from Lauren, but the last thing I wanted to think about was that article right now and her editing notes. So I closed that one and clicked on the one from Marcus Hadley. He was a sports editor who I worked with in college when I covered the college football. We also went to high school together but didn't know each other that well. More like passing acquaintances. He was also friends with Silas back then. Not great, because believe me when I say I begged him for information back then and he had none as to why Silas left.

Marcus basically asked how I was doing and if I had any leads on sports articles I could write for his blog. I told him I would keep an eye out for potential leads. This wasn't unusual for him. I usually heard from him every few months looking for stories he could feature.

It was nearing five and I could already feel the anxiety of working out. It shouldn't be dreaded, should it?

I bet no one likes working out. Only crazy people. It's like they're brainwashed.

Around four, Destry called and said he was running late and wouldn't be able to meet me at the bar until seven thirty. Believe me when I say I was okay with that. In fact, I tried to get out of it even.

"I'm really sore." I said. "Maybe I should take a day's break."

Destry was quiet for a moment, my heart thudded waiting for his response. And then it came and I wasn't pleased.

"Yeah, I figured you would quit."

The nerve of this asshole. That pissed me off. Who was he to fucking judge me on being sore?

"See you at seven thirty." I hung up and didn't wait for a reply. Screw him.

When I got there, Destry was in the basement sitting on the floor against the wall staring at his phone. I was ten minutes late and he wasn't impressed.

I tried to be enthusiastic when I walked in and not act like I was dying from muscle fatigue but I wasn't very convincing.

Destry saw right through my fake enthusiasm. "I hope you're here to work out. Don't be wasting my fucking time."

I was done with his shit. I wasn't paying him to be treated like this. "Jesus, what's your deal, man? Why are you so mean?"

"You called me for help." He gave a huff and started slamming weights around. "This isn't something where you get to know me. So don't bother."

"Okay," I nodded smiling, "so you're always a dick?"

"Pretty much. Get used to it." He motioned toward the weights. "Grab a weight that feels comfortable and follow what I do."

We started out with some stretches, in which I stared at the wall and refused to look at him.

"Now go grab a weight."

I did as he said and stood next to him. There was about a foot of space between us but I could feel his body heat that close, and smell him. So good. Like sweat and some kind of cologne. It made me want to dig through that gym bag and find it so I could buy some just to smell. Unconsciously, I smelled him.

Of course he noticed, gave me a look, something between a glare and confusion, and then rolled his eyes.

He rolled his fucking eyes at me.

I felt like he insulted me—which he more than likely did—but I ignored him anyways.

"You know what a lunge is, right?"

I bet if I dropped this weight on his foot it could break his toe. I wouldn't even feel bad. *Go ahead Tallan, drop the weight.*

I crossed my arms over my chest, glowering at him. "Yes." I replied, trying to sound annoyed. I didn't exactly have to try too hard either. Fuck enthusiasm.

"Alright, follow my lead then." Destry made one step with his right leg, and squatted down until he was at a ninety degree angle. Then he rose, and did the same thing with his left leg, all the while walking toward the brick wall. He had good posture and his legs looked like solid muscles. I couldn't help but stare. If he wasn't such a dick, I'd be attracted to him.

He turned to look back at me. "What are you waiting for?"

I didn't answer. Instead I put my head down and started walking toward the wall.

We continued like that, alternating lunges and squats, and then he got out the jump rope.

"Just start out basic here. But jumping rope is great for cardio." He said, beginning a pace that seemed slow for him, but would have me panting in ten seconds.

I looked up at him and watched the way it looked so effortless for him and the way his muscles looked in his arms as he moved the rope with a simple twist of his wrists.

Stop staring at him.

I did as he said but the problem was everything joggled so much I couldn't focus on anything but my boobs bouncing around and the way I must have looked.

It wasn't like Destry was even paying any attention to me though. He just stared at the wall. In reality, a girl like me wouldn't even be on his radar.

While I was visibly panting, he stopped and motioned for me to continue. "Do that for five minutes. Then do the lunges, squats, and jump rope again. Keep that up for thirty minutes."

And then he disappeared again.

I could have stopped. He wouldn't have known but I would. To motivate myself I put on some music. All Silas Cade songs, of course. I didn't care for his last album but the one he released two years ago, the one that got him that number one spot on the Billboard 100, was my favorite. It kept me moving for sure. Imagining him singing it to me, I kinda got in the groove and before I knew it the next 30 minutes had passed me by.

That's when Destry appeared again. Without much grace, he ripped out my headphones. "Let's go for a run."

"It's like nine at night." I grabbed my ear and glared. That hurt. "No one runs in Seattle at night."

He stopped and walked backwards scrunching his eyebrows at me. "Says who?"

He didn't wait for my answer before he was walking toward the door.

Rubbing my ear where he ripped out the headphones, I gathered my phone up and set it by my bag. I touched my ear once more when I approached him. "Do you have to be so damn rough? That pulled my hair."

He turned, never making eye contact with me and rolled his eyes. He didn't give a shit.

He had no fucking manners at all.

Like Catie said, how he actually kept a girlfriend was beyond me.

I didn't want to be left alone in that basement so I followed him up the stairs. "Leave the music." He ordered when I reached for my phone again.

So no manners and demanding. That's what I was working with.

I followed, not sure what this would be like. I wasn't a runner. Unless you count running from the bus to my apartment because I was afraid of the dark. That's how I run. A full on life or death sprint knowing I just had to be faster than the elderly to save myself. I'd watched *The Walking Dead*, those who ran just had to be faster than one other person. Some called it survival of the fittest, in my case it was survival of the fattest.

Surely we'd need to pace ourselves.

When we got outside, there was a steady mist but it felt nice. Almost relaxing, but still, not exactly what I had in mind.

Wrapping my arms around my waist, I pulled at my shirt that was clinging to my already sweaty body. Destry noticed immediately and gave me another look and watched me fidget with my clothing. He made me so nervous.

"Have you ever ran before?" He looked over his shoulder up the street when someone honked and called his name out their window, and then back at me.

"Well, yeah… " I gave him a stupid look.

"I mean like five miles."

"Oh yeah," I waved my arms around, "when I was training for a marathon last month."

Not even a smile. He never found my jokes funny. Not that I was trying to be funny, but Jesus, crack a smile every once in a while.

And then he said, "Yeah, sure you have," rolling his eyes yet again.

I would love to throw a few punches to this guy. Maybe I could pound some laughs back into him.

Destry didn't wait for me before he started walking up Alaskan Way and then began a slow jog. I watched his ass. I'm not sure why, but I did and it was nice.

He's sexy. And he knows it.

And I sound like a rap song now. Or pop. Whatever. The point is Destry knew the appeal he held.

Between his ass and his muscles in his back, I wasn't exactly jogging. When he was out of sight, I had no choice but to go after him.

It wasn't bad at first. I did wonder if my own ass had bruises from all the shaking. It was awful. I would have to see what it looked like from behind.

Destry turned around about twenty feet ahead of me, jogging backwards. "Tallan?"

Call me crazy but I pretended I didn't hear him so he would say my name again in that velvet smooth voice of his when it was somewhat winded. "Tallan?"

God. Damn. It was like what it would sound like if we were having sex. I bet, at least.

What? Why are you even thinking that? This guy is a total tool, don't think that way around him.

"You coming?"

Not yet, boxer boy, but I bet you could get me there! Damn, why am I thinking this shit about this asshole?

I couldn't actually speak at that point. I couldn't even catch my breath let alone utter a monosyllabic response. I hoped we were heading past Harborview Medical Center because I would sneak inside and get some oxygen. Or pass out.

Destry slowed his pace more and waited. "Remember to breathe. Take slow even breaths."

Slow even breaths. This wasn't my first time having sex. This was much more intense.

We made it to what seemed like another ten miles when we ended up back at the bar. I had no idea what direction we went, where, or how long that had taken. I couldn't think because all my blood was going to my legs.

"How far did we go?" I asked with my hands resting on my knees as I used the building to hold me up. I could feel my face on fire to the point where my sweat was actually cooling me off.

"Maybe a mile." I stood and held my side like I'd been stabbed. I was sweating so bad my hair was falling in my face, muscles and lungs burning like each breath might be my last. "Well, shit."

He laughed.

Destry.

Stone.

Laughed.

The smile was barely visible but then the sound and smile faded just as easily as it came. He lifted his dark gray t-shirt to wipe the sweat from his own face. My eyes immediately went to the visible tan skin that peeked its way out.

Holy mother. Look at that guy's stomach!

He caught me looking but didn't say anything. For a moment, there seemed to be an awkward silence between us and then he shrugged. "Make sure you stretch out your muscles before bed and drink plenty of water tonight and tomorrow."

Then he left, no more words, nothing. He disappeared inside the bar while I went downstairs through the other door to retrieve my bag.

He was so weird.

On the way back to my apartment, I could barely walk. It hurt so bad.

I wanted to murder the person who decided it was a good idea to invent stairs. No seriously, fuck you stair inventor. That's exactly what I would say to them.

Chapter Five
OUTSIDE FIGHTER

An outside fighter or range fighter tries to maintain that gap between himself and his opponent, fighting with longer range punches. Outside fighters have to be fast on their feet, stepping in with a jab and stepping back out of range quickly to evade their opponent.

When I got home that night I wasn't pleased. Not only could I not walk, but Destry was kind of a dick. And for the sake of my jiggly ass, I kept enduring the pain.

The door was unlocked and I wondered why Jared gave me such shit but he could leave it unlocked.

"How come you don't lock it and I have to?" I asked knowing he was more than likely laying on the couch.

Yep. There he was drinking a beer. "Because I have a gun and you don't." Jared said holding up his gun on the coffee table in front of him. I was tempted to snatch the beer from him. What I would give for a beer right now.

His eyes were still on the television but when he did look at me, he laughed. I'm sure I looked like death, or something fairly similar.

"Wow."

"Shut up. Don't say anything to me unless it's nice. I want coffee, I can't move and I'm dying for some fucking sugar."

Running his hands over his face, Jared sat up. "You can't have sugar?"

"I shouldn't, right?" I sat down beside him and then sniffed my armpits. It almost knocked me out. How Destry hadn't said anything was beyond me. "I smell awful."

"Yes, you do..." He scrunched his nose and scooted a foot away.

"Usually you can't have sugar when you're dieting but I think you need some. Don't cut it out completely."

"No, I need to lose weight." My words came out completely defeated. Much like I felt. "I'm staying away from it."

Jared gave me that look. "Don't starve yourself."

"I know." I changed the subject. No need to talk about my issues this late. "How was work?"

"It was all right." Jared rolled his eyes. "I'll be glad when I'm off patrol. I arrested some douche for beatin' the crap out of a girl. He was nineteen and she was his sixteen-year-old girlfriend."

"Whoa." I looked over at him. "Heavy."

"Yeah, dude's got issues. I remember him back when I did my ride along in college. He'd just gotten out of child protective services and is now just stayin' in the system."

"Sounds like it."

We sat there staring at the TV when Jared looked over at me, his head rolled to the side like he was exhausted. "So what's the champ doing?"

"Ex-champ. And he's a douche. I bet he's BFF's with that guy you arrested today."

"Doubt that."

"I wouldn't. He's got this 'I'm angry and used' attitude that makes me want to punch him myself. I don't understand why he's so bitter."

"It sounds like he's had a lot of people use him over the years."

It was my turn to roll my eyes. "Like who?"

"Danny said his girl did. Apparently he lost that fight to Ray Lucas and she left him right after he lost the fight."

"That's rough." I still didn't feel bad for him. No way. My body hurt too bad to have any sort of sympathy for anyone other than myself.

I definitely imagined Destry had a girl. Or had one. A guy that looked like him most certainly had girls when he wanted them. Those green eyes alone could bag him a chick if not for the dark lashes that seemed to give just the right shadows over them. Then there was the jaw line and rigid muscles. Oh yeah, he could most definitely get any woman he wanted.

Jared smiled and flicked my ear. The sore one. "Are you already having fantasies about Destry?"

Lie. Because you know damn well you are.

"Ugh!" I pushed myself up from the couch. "I am not." I lied. "He's such an asshole."

I kept saying that but there's no way I believed it entirely after hearing him laugh. There was a good side to Destry. Deep down there had to be.

Once again, that night I couldn't sleep. My thoughts were going from Silas to Destry and back again.

Why was I doing this for one night?

Easy. Silas Cade.

I checked Twitter since that's where I frequently stalked Silas once I found out he had Twitter. He didn't update too often but he had posted a tweet three hours ago.

@SilasCade Less than 6 weeks and I'm headin' home. Feels good. Can't wait to see familiar faces.

Was he talking about me?

He had to be.

My heart started pounding as a smile appeared. He was talking about me. I knew it.

He didn't have Facebook other than a fan page which he never posted on but his bandmates sometimes did. So I couldn't properly stalk him there. Or I would have.

Then, I typed in Destry Stone.

What the fuck is wrong with you?

Not that I expected him to have Twitter or anything. Not surprisingly, he didn't. But there was a ton of shit on there about him. Mostly gossip.

He was talked about even four months after that fight. For a good hour I sat there trolling through months of tweets that ragged on him. There were some that were on his side and spoke highly of him and his fighting style, which was said to be aggressive but with back-alley speed and patience that was unheard of for someone who was only twenty-four. Though he came out swinging, he'd measure his opponent. Study them.

There was nothing about Destry after the fight. He avoided the press and his only comment over and over was, "I want a fucking rematch."

I clicked on a link where they talked to the guy he fought, Ray Lucas, and he said, "If he wants a rematch, I'll give him one. He's a respectable guy and lands a mean punch. He's also hittable. Going into the fight everyone said I wouldn't get a hit on him. I did. I knocked him out too. He's not invincible."

There wasn't a lot of information surrounding the fight in December. After reading all that and how the public had harassed him and accused him of throwing the fight, I almost felt bad for him. Almost.

As I sat there reading, one thing was very evident. My body hurt, I was starving and I wanted to quit. So because of that I didn't feel bad for him. Shockingly, the only thing keeping me from quitting at that point was Destry. Surprisingly. And not even in the sense that I liked him as Jared suspected. I most certainly didn't.

I just didn't want to hear I told you so from him. Call me stubborn but that was me.

In a way, having Destry around was a good thing whether I wanted to admit it or not.

Saturday
April 9, 2011

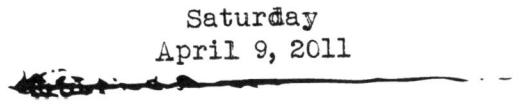

The next morning, guess what? I couldn't move again. It was becoming a tradition of sorts. Only problem was I felt like I still hadn't recovered from the first work-out. And my left calf hurt so bad, like I'd pulled a muscle in it. I'd heard rumors that the second day after you start working out is the worst. I could testify to that fact. I only *thought* I couldn't move yesterday…today, the shit was real.

So there I laid wishing death upon myself. Or maybe my own

personal massage therapist who made house calls.

I bet Destry gives a good massage.

What the fuck is wrong with you? Lock that shit down, Tallan. Don't even think like that.

My phone beeped so I twisted, which was a horrible idea. New levels of pain assaulted my already beaten body. Even my ears hurt this morning. Probably because Destry ripped out my hair last night when he so rudely removed my headphones.

It was a text from him telling me to meet him at the gym at eight tonight and drink plenty of water today. Even though it was Saturday, he said we needed to get in five full days each week which meant I could take Tuesdays and Wednesdays off. It really was starting to feel like boot camp. I was looking forward to Tuesday.

I got out of bed, okay, I rolled over to the edge of the bed and just fell into the floor. Thank you, Jesus, for inventing gravity because falling required no effort. I crawled out of my bedroom. Same difference. I made it to the kitchen, used the cabinets and counters to stand and retrieved a glass.

"Here's to day three of my workout." I said, filling a glass of water.

After that, I had no choice but to get dressed since I had to go see Lauren this morning, finish the edits for that article and then I needed to spend some time at the library doing research on solar energy.

Any time spent doing research flies by for me. I'm very much into research. While I was there I did what I probably shouldn't have done.

I did some research on Destry. I couldn't help myself.

What surprised me was what popped up on Google first. Stella Summers. The alleged girlfriend I met the other night.

Who names their daughter Stella? Obviously her parents were fans of *A Streetcar Named Desire* because what other reason would there be for burdening your child with that dated name. Did they not think that one through? Clearly not.

Unless they were setting her up to be a future stripper. That was an option—based on her appearance and demeanor—that held great potential.

January 2011 - TMZ

The situation for Destry Stone couldn't get any more awkward than seeing your girl walk out during the fight you just lost with your opponent. During the fight the small town girl who captured the fighter's attention two years ago was seen crossing her arms and looking the other direction as the fight unfolded, visibly upset at Stone's performance.

It was the fifth round when Stone went down by way of a knockout and Summers walked.

A source close to the couple said the high-profile pair had apparently been on the rocks for the last year. Stone has made no public comment regarding their split and refused when asked to comment during a press conference held a week after the fight saying it was, "None of our fucking business."

Okay, so it's true. He's unattached. Or maybe this wasn't true and just something they printed. I knew not to completely trust everything I read online.

There were photographs of this Stella Summers and I had a feeling they didn't do this girl justice. It was like the photos of Silas I would find. I knew the effect Silas had on me in person. And I also knew a photo couldn't capture that.

It was nearly six that night by the time I left the library much like my time spent on trolling last night, it was a vortex of time I got sucked into and hours later re-emerged. I got home with enough time to grab some food, a piece of chicken Jared made last night and then I shoved some carrots in my mouth. Topped that off with a string cheese. Clearly I wasn't eating that great. But I did drink plenty of water. And peed hopefully my weight in the water I was drinking.

Being a Saturday night, the bar was packed. Cars lined the gravel parking lot along with a handful of patrons sitting on their hoods smoking. When I walked past them, aroused whistles permeated the air but I kept walking with my head down. You don't pay attention to that shit in Seattle. A woman walking alone towards a bar had bad idea written all over it. I certainly wasn't dressed for a classy establishment such as this, hell, on second thought, maybe I was. After all, the entrance reeked of piss.

I walked into the bar and headed towards the basement stairs. In my own way, this was my walk of shame. I knew the pain and suffering I was going to endure and the thought of Destry and his rudeness towards me made this torturous event even less appealing. I learned from the last two days that Destry went out of his way to be rude. But he did smile at me last night. So what changed?

I walked down to the basement to await my torture, Destry was in the same spot he was last night, waiting for me against the wall. He looked a little different tonight. Angry yeah, but something seemed different. His mood was noticeably different. I was almost afraid to approach him. I thought I was dreading tonight but seeing his demeanor, I actually started shaking. Whatever was going on with him was going to be taken out on me tonight.

I stayed in my place, almost afraid to approach him. I looked down at him, not sure what to say. I knew I was a few minutes late but I don't think my punctuality would cause this reaction. Something else was definitely going on. Maybe he had another visit from his ex and that has put him in a foul mood…yet, when I did briefly make eye contact, there was something more brimming just at the edges of his eyes. Sadness almost. He immediately looked back at his hands, almost like he didn't want me seeing what was really going on. Nah, sadness couldn't be it. This dude was as emotionless as the brick wall he was leaned up against. Whatever it was, I was scared…for *me* and my aching body.

He stood, his arms steadying himself against the brick wall. He stared at the ground as he spoke, but then slowly lifted his eyes to mine. There was so much emotion in them I was caught off guard. Until he spoke. "Nice of you to show up."

He doesn't waste any time does he?

"Can you just be pleasant for one day?"

Destry rolled his eyes as I watched him walk toward the mats on the basement floor.

Ten minutes later he had me doing sit-ups. I hate sit-ups. I understand what they do and the general idea but it doesn't make my stomach muscles grateful, it just makes them pissed. And it hurt my neck.

"You're not doing them right." Destry said when he noticed me struggling. He seemed calmer when he spoke but still had that tense edge. "You're supposed to lift your shoulders off the ground and keep your chin raised up. Don't tuck it down to your chest."

What he failed to understand was that my chin being tucked towards my chest was the only way I was getting my body off this mat towards my knees. Call my chin action the gas in my engine. Without this position, my body would stall and I'd lay on the mat like a wilted fat flower.

But I attempted to do as he said, only he had to demonstrate. I knew exactly what was about to happen. He was going to touch me. My entire body tensed in anticipation.

My nipples hardened. And he was in a prime spot to get my full on high beams right in his face.

Destry got down beside me on his knees and with no hesitation, he reached out and placed two fingers under my chin to raise it up, rough skin sliding across mine. Then he took his palm and placed it on my shoulders. "Cross your arms over your chest," then he moved to hold my feet kneeling between my legs.

Oh God, he's at my feet. If I opened my legs right now his head would be between my legs.

Open your legs!

No. Don't.

His voice was low and controlled. "Tighten your stomach muscles by drawing in your belly button." His eyes lifted from my stomach to my eyes, a moment of silence fell over us. Then he moved his hand to my stomach and flattened it.

Sweet Jesus. Move your hand lower. Lower, damn it!

I felt every single finger on my skin with just the slightest pressure.

Just a little lower and keep that pressure.

What the hell is wrong with me?

"Keep your stomach tight, feet on the ground, then slowly lift your head followed by your shoulder blades until you're at a ninety degree angle." He put his other hand on my feet as I raised my body up. "Hold that position for a minute and then bring your torso back to the floor." He watched me, his impassive eyes dark concentrating on my form. When I did as he said, he smiled. Actually smiled. "Good. Do that twenty more times and then I'll show you another set."

I did, and then he proceeded to show me five different kinds of sit-ups. Who knew there was more than one?

Thirty minutes into that we stopped to drink some water before he was going to show me back exercises. I was silently hoping there was more touching. I could only gather that this mental change in my previous thoughts of him being an asshole to now wanting, hell, silently begging for him to put his hands on me had something to do with lack of food and the lactic acid that was being released from my screaming muscles. It was messing with my brain.

We were standing near the wall of weights when he looked over at me, his eyes examining my face, as if he was trying to decide on what he wanted to say. "Ordinarily a person wouldn't go through this much just for one night."

Everyone thought I was crazy for doing this but I had my reasons. They were just that. Mine. As in, I shouldn't have to explain myself.

"What if one night gave you an answer that finally made sense?" I asked, shifting my weight and leaning into the wall as I tried to stretch my calf muscles that were cramping up so bad.

He didn't give my question any thought. At least I didn't think he did. "So what, you win tickets or something to be a groupie?"

"No." I snorted, trying to appear annoyed. I didn't have to try very hard. "I used to date him in high school."

Destry raised an eyebrow, a small twist of his lips, then shook his head without saying anything, his eyes focused on the water bottle in his hands. Standing straight, he motioned toward a bench near the wall and retrieved a pair of free weights.

"You don't believe me?" I took the weights from him and sat on the bench.

He lifted his eyes to mine considering the question and then wiped the back of his hand over his jaw as if he had an itch. Motherfucker didn't have an itch.

"I don't care." His eyes then dropped back down to my hands.

My jaw dropped. Literally. "What?"

When he shrugged, I wanted to once again, shove this weight in my hand up his ass. Here I am trying to reserve judgment about him and be nice for today, but the more I'm around him, the more I understand this guy is just an all-around dick.

"I said I don't care." He kept his head down as he spoke. "I don't give a shit that you used to date him, fuck him, follow him around like a stalker, I don't really care."

You're an ass.

Now I didn't say this, only because a guy like Destry already knew this. There's absolutely no sense in telling him.

I just continued with the workout. I had a goal, I didn't need his opinions or his judgment. Fuck him and his high horse.

Sunday
April 10, 2011

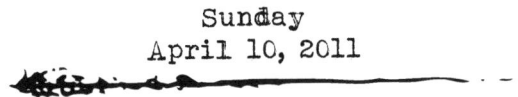

Before my work out on Sunday, I met Marcus for brunch at Tilikum Place Café. It was one of my favorite places to eat. My morning started off good. It's a given that I was sore but when I pulled on a pair of jeans, they suddenly didn't feel too tight. How cool was that? It had only been a few torturous days but this definitely made the pain bearable.

I took the bus to the restaurant. When I walked in, Marcus was already seated at a table in the corner. Sunday's were always busy here, crowded and usually an hour wait. Luckily Marcus was always prepared and had made reservations.

I smiled as I approached him. He did the same, stood and wrapped his skinny arms around mine. Marcus was tall but had a lanky build, brown eyes and dark hair that fell in his face. Very different from the man I was hanging out with these days.

"So, Tallan," Marcus took a seat folding the napkin on the table on his lap, "what have you been up to?"

"Not much." I did the same, sitting across from him and then raised my water glass to my lips and took a drink. A few drops fell down my chin as I gracefully attempted to rid my face of the fact that water wasn't my drink of choice. "Hired a personal trainer to get my ass in shape."

Marcus laughed as I wiped away the water. Only he wasn't laughing about me being in a constant state of disarray and always spilling everything. By the bright-eyed look, he was entertained by the idea that I was working out. I didn't really think this was funny.

Why did people laugh when I said this?

"You look fine to me. Why would you do that?"

"Denial. You're in denial." I motioned to my ass barely fitting in my jeans. "I didn't get like this by accident. Anyhow, I'm meeting Silas in a few weeks and I wanted to look good."

He looked down at the menu one last time. "You've been talking about him for years, that's good to finally get closure, right?"

"That's my hope anyways."

We ordered our meals. I kept myself under control and ordered a veggie omelet and orange juice. I wasn't sure I could have orange juice but I was dying for some. Marcus gave me a look because he knew when we came here I devoured a plate of pancakes. Not now though. I'm a woman on a mission.

Marcus shook his head brushing his brown thick hair from his eyes. "So what have you been working on?"

"Lunges."

He smiled his crooked smile. Marcus could be considered cute but I'd never really given much thought to it. Kind of like Jared. It was just never going to happen. "I meant on your articles."

"Oh, that." Of course he was talking about work. He's a very task oriented person. This is so funny to me because he's good friends with

Jared now since they met in college, his complete opposite. "Mostly city council articles. Just finished up an article on the Seattle Light Rail Project. I've got two articles I'm working on for various blogs but what do you have in mind?"

"What do you know about Destry Stone?"

I sighed. Somehow I knew the conversation would go this way. "Jared told you, didn't he?"

His head tipped back from laughing. Jerk. "Yeah, well he said you were working out with him."

"See, he's worse than a fucking girl. Can't keep his mouth shut. I bet he told you about cutting me out of my jeans too, didn't he."

Marcus smiled, still laughing but looked down at his food that had just arrived. "He may have mentioned something like that."

"He's such an asshole."

"Who, Jared or Destry?"

"Well, both really. But Jared right now." I leaned forward resting my hands on the table. "I'm going to kick his ass. And now that I'm getting in shape, I'm just the person to do it too!"

And then like a switch was flipped, something he's so good at, his face is suddenly serious. "About Destry... how well do you know him?"

I took a moment to think about the question and cut into my omelet. How well did I know him?

I didn't.

"He's my personal trainer but he's about as closed off as a safe."

Marcus frowned, squinting his eyes. "I know you. A challenge is good. How do you feel about writing an article about him? Something to profile him as a local guy."

"Good or bad? I've heard mixed feelings about him and after spending a week with him, I'm understanding the bad."

"That's the thing, Tallan." Marcus relaxes in his chair taking a drink of his coffee. "No one knows for sure what happened with that fight." He set the cup down and stared at me. "Only Destry. I'd kinda like to leave it up to you on this one. Write the article on how you see it flowing once you find out more about him and what happened."

Write the article? How the hell am I going to do that? It's not like the guy has said more than five words to me that don't involve the words reps, squats, lunges, and don't waste my time.

"So basically do the research, talk to him and write what I feel happened to cause him to not get in the boxing ring professionally anymore?"

"Yeah, I'm certain you'll find the answer everyone's looking for." Marcus reached for the check when the waiter brought it by. "He won't talk to reporters and knocked out the last person who tried to do a story on him."

I started digging through my bag for money. "Oh fabulous, that makes me feel better." I handed him a twenty only to have him push it back at me.

"He's not going to do that to you." He held up his credit card. "And I've got this."

"So you say, have you met him?"

Marcus laughed again. "I can attest to his left hook, yeah."

"So you're the one he knocked out?" I laughed so hard causing a new pain in my ribs to emerge. I don't know why Marcus' revelation about him being the one who got tagged by Destry was so funny to me. And it wasn't the first time Marcus had been knocked out trying to get information out of people. But, yeah, that was hysterical.

"Sadly, yes. Down for the fucking count."

Part of me, okay, all of me wasn't thrilled about getting to know Destry better for the simple fact that he'd been such a douche to me so far. I was okay with working out and not venturing into the friend zone with him. Writing this article meant I'd have to ask him questions in roundabout ways and judging by the interactions we've had so far, this wasn't going to be easy at all.

I decided to walk back to my apartment and not only get a little exercise since my legs were so sore, maybe warm them up a little and it was a beautiful day in the city. Felt like it was at least in the sixties and not a cloud to be seen.

When I got home from brunch and my walk, Catie was in our apartment, with the door unlocked, and Jared was apparently in the shower. If I was in here, Jared would have went ape shit to know the door was unlocked.

"He bitches at me but yet the door is unlocked yet again." I locked the door behind me when I got inside the apartment. "What are you doing here?"

Catie rolled her eyes but continued to watch whatever movie she had on. She was sitting in the chair closest to the balcony with the door open. The breeze was actually nice for once. Kind of felt good to have fresh air in the place. Spring in Seattle was one of my favorite times of year, when it wasn't raining, which was more often than not. Seattle natives had to take advantage of days like this as much as we could.

After grabbing a bottle of water from the fridge, I sat next to Catie. "Hey, you remember that sports editor I knew in college, Marcus?"

"Yeah, I think." Catie thought for a moment. "Yeah, I do. Jared's friends with him, right?"

"Yes." I glared. "Anyways, he was asking around about a story on Destry. He suggested I do a story on him. Help him get his name back."

"You hate him." She pointed out when Jared appeared around the corner without a shirt. "Why would you want to help him?"

"I'm not even sure. There's just something about him that I find… interesting." I looked over at Jared and then stood to jam my finger in his chest. "And you, asshole. Why did you tell Marcus you had to cut me out of my jeans?"

"Because that shit was probably the funniest thing I've participated in all year." Jared stepped back and pulled a t-shirt over his head. "You ready to go, Catie?"

"And here I thought you were my friend, instead you've probably blabbed to everyone about my skinny jeans fiasco."

"Ummmm…how many people count as everyone? And they can

only be classified as skinny jeans if you can get them on and off and, well…"

Oh, holy hell, Jared is a dead man!

"Where are you two going?"

"Lunch."

"Dating, huh?"

Jared glared at me. "No, just going to get food."

"Fucking each other and food." I smiled at them, both watching each other to see if one was going to react. "That's considered dating in some cultures and in other cultures it's just considered friends with benefits …so which is it?"

Jared reached out and pushed me. I didn't have great balance and fell back on the couch. "Says the girl who is thinking about her personal trainer in dirty ways."

Catie laughed as they headed for the door. "Should I start looking for a place to stay? Are you moving in together soon?"

Jared flung his arm up behind his head and flipped me off when he got to the door. Then he stopped before closing the door. "Yeah, ask the champ. I'm sure he's got room in his ring for you."

Ask the champ, my ass.

Shit. How the hell am I going to write this article?

Ordinarily I have no problems writing whatever. I'm good under pressure and digging into topics that aren't covered too often. Lately I've been more on the political side of news. This would be entirely different. In a strange way, I was looking forward to the challenge of it. If there's one thing I knew for sure, Destry Stone was the biggest challenge of all.

I met Destry at the bar around five that night. He said we had to be finished by seven so he could meet someone. Part of me wondered if he had a date but no way was I going to ask that just yet. I'd have to work up to this with him.

"I'm down an entire jean size," I said, almost conversationally to him. "How'd that happen in a week?"

Destry shrugged as we stretched out our muscles on the mats. "Water weight probably but sometimes the first ten pounds come off quickly."

"I'll be a size six before I know it!" Reaching forward I pressed my chest into my leg to stretch out my calf that had been bothering me.

"There's absolutely nothing wrong with a woman who wears a size ten, Tallan." Destry said, shaking his head and standing. "Real woman have curves. They shouldn't be limited and defined by a fuckin' number."

"You shouldn't be in here." Danny said following a blonde babe down the stairs. I watched her walk toward Destry with a slow strut.

Destry, who had finished stretching was over by the weights and turned to look over his shoulder, his body immediately tensed.

"Stay out of it, Danny." Destry glared at her immediately, taking one step toward her. "What are you doing here?"

"Came to give you your key back."

He smiled at her, that full on grin he had. The one I'd only seen once. Only it was clear it was forced. "Nice of you."

She sighed and I could tell their parting wasn't pleasant. Her hand went to her hip. "Don't be an asshole."

Destry held up his hands, smiling in a condescending way that I recognized. He was getting ready to be an asshole. "I said, nice of you."

He held out his hand to take the key and she dropped it on the floor. "Have a good day, champ."

He winked at her, picked the key up and threw it against the wall. It pinged as it made contact and then fell to the concrete floor. "You too," he turned to walk away, "Stella."

Oh God, that was Stella? Holy. Shit. Look at her!

When I saw Stella, a few things went through my mind. Again, why would anyone name their daughter Stella Summer? Were they high?

And then my next thought was damn, I wasn't even on the competition radar compared with a girl like her.

But Destry was right. He liked women. Real women. Stella was a woman. Long legs, huge tits, curves, just downright stunning.

He walked back over to me when she left, his posture and mood much like it was last night, different and tensed.

"Who is that girl?"

"Ex-girlfriend." He mumbled staring at his phone now in his hand.

"Oh, wow, she's pretty." I was trying to be kind, but I failed to realize that wasn't what he wanted to hear right then.

He glared, eyes flashing with annoyance that I even spoke to him right then. And by glare I mean he looked like he wanted to murder me for saying that.

Okay, well apparently we don't talk about that.

His stare made me nervous. Made me want to run from him before I even knew anything more about him based on the anger behind that stare. Somewhere, somehow, someone had fucked this guy up emotionally. In fact, emotionally damaged doesn't do this guy justice. Emotionally devastated might.

"We're done for the day." He said, still staring at me.

"What? All we did was stretch." He couldn't be serious, could he? No workout all because of that girl?

"I said we're fuckin' done." By the way he spoke to me, it was as if I wasn't even worth his time to explain. "We'll pick up tomorrow."

That pissed me off. "I'm paying you to train me, not blow me off."

Destry laughed and walked toward the stairs, leaving. "Then don't come back. Wouldn't bother me at all."

Was he fucking serious?

By the door slamming behind him, he was.

Monday
April 11, 2011

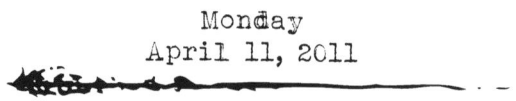

I can't say I was pleased about last night and what happened between Destry and me after Stella left. I think I hated the guy more now than I did when I first met him. Like the hate was festering. He called late last night and asked that we workout in the morning because he had plans that night. I said okay but didn't say much else.

"Alright, I have a few rules we should have talked about earlier." He didn't waste any time going into them either when I got to the bar. "Don't ask me personal questions."

"And?"

He didn't look at me when he spoke, instead he stared at the ring to his left. "Don't waste my time."

Why did he have to be so weird all the time?

"Got it. But let's be honest here, you wasted my time last night."

"I'm sorry about that. It won't happen again."

Say what? Destry Stone knows how to apologize? Have the stars aligned?

I would have thanked him for at least acknowledging that he was wrong but I was so annoyed with him at that point I didn't really give a flying fuck about Destry Stone's life, or that he apologized. I didn't want to know anything and I was going to tell Marcus exactly that when I saw him later tonight.

We were an hour into the workout when all the water I had been drinking these days caught up to me.

I had to pee. Oh my God, did I have to pee.

I had no choice but to use that bathroom I swore I'd never use.

Have you ever used a port-a-potty? Okay. So imagine that but after four days in hundred degree weather after a concert. That might give you an understanding of what that bathroom resembled.

By the time I got back I was ready to vomit and for some reason, Destry was smiling again. "What's with that face?"

"That bathroom smells like someone died in there."

He shrugged. "Someone probably did," and then he cracked a smile, "There's a locker room. You could have used that."

"There's a locker room?"

His eyes brightened as he spoke. "Yeah, with a shower too."

I threw my towel at him. "You motherfucker."

He did nothing but shake his head and toss the towel on the ground.

"Come on, let's go for a run."

I wasn't looking forward to a run but at least I could get some fresh air and maybe get that smell out of my nose from the bathroom.

"Who is that guy?" I asked when I saw a man come downstairs and set a bag near the ring.

Destry looked over his shoulder at the dark skinned man standing to his left. "Adam. My trainer."

"A trainer with a trainer?" I'll admit I was amused with my comebacks this morning.

Destry was not. I took the weight in my hands and started doing those horrendous hammer curls.

He snorted, almost disgusted as he grumbled words. "Like you don't know who I am."

"Well, I suppose I know of you, *champ.*"

His eyes moved slowly around the basement and landed on the ring, processing what I said to him. He walked past me with a scowl, his shoulder bumping mine. "Thought so. Let's go."

Chapter Six

GO TO THE SCORECARDS

Go to the scorecards means that after a fight has gone its scheduled number of rounds the judges' score cards will determine the winner. It is also used when there is a fight stoppage due to an accidental head butt if the fight has gone beyond 4 rounds.

Destry and I finished our run that morning, went a mile and a half before I tried to convince him to just drop me off at the hospital. It would be easier that way since I couldn't breathe. At all.

It wasn't entirely from the run either. It was from the stretching afterwards. Yeah, stretching with Destry can and will make you breathless.

"Here, let me help you." Destry said, grabbing my hands to help me stretch out my calf. It hurt like hell after the run. He had me sit down on the mat and prop my leg up on the stool he sat down on.

When he touched my bare legs that I thankfully shaved this morning, shivers ran up my spine. Destry swallowed – with difficulty – it seemed. As soon as he touched me, I flinched.

He let out a small laugh trailing his hands up my leg. For a moment his eyes were trained on mine until I blinked and he dropped them back down to his hands massaging my calf. He had long fingers. Really long, strong, masculine hands that I imagined could get a good grip on you. There went my mind.

I shifted, uncomfortably when his thumbs started a slow motion against my calf muscle. Not only did it hurt, but I wanted his hands higher, and I had no idea why.

He was an asshole. Why I was having dirty thoughts about him was confusing to me.

It's because you haven't had sex in close to a year. That's why.

Yeah, there's that. Nothing was said at first. I wasn't sure he was going to say anything at all. Wouldn't surprise me either.

"How's that?" Destry's voice was quiet, a smile playing at his lips, but delivered in a way that made my body tremble. I felt like when he spoke the words were delivered in a way that made you realize they were carefully chosen.

"Good…" I nearly moaned, my eyes fading shut slightly. No, scratch that, I all out moaned the sound of arousal and he knew it. He felt my reaction to his touch. He had to have known what he was doing to me.

He cleared his throat, shifting slightly on the stool. One thing I noticed right then was his attention. It was as though he was studying me. And when his eyes dropped, I understood it was very much focused on what he was doing.

I wanted to say something, maybe thank him for being nice for once, but I didn't. Instead I was momentarily shocked that he was touching me in that way. Or at all. This was Destry we were talking about.

After a moment, his eyes lifted to mine as I remained motionless before him. There was so much I could have said to him right then. Most of it would have been snarky and probably upset him. In no way did I want him to stop. The way his fingertips felt and the way the muscle in his forearms moved was almost too much to take.

"You look deep in thought." He mused.

Uh, hello. I'm thinking about you moving those sexy strong hands higher. Of course I'm lost in thought.

"It hurts."

"Do you want me to stop?" His voice was low, and I let out another breathy sound.

"No, it feels good." I felt my spine arch, my breasts on display for him.

He looked. Destry was never shy about looking, even from day one. He continued and curled his fingers around my calf. I wanted to reach out and feel his forearms and run my hands over his chest. Then

I wanted to thread that thick dark hair between my fingers and run my hands down that sharp scruffy jaw line.

Destry's mouth quirked into a small smile, running his eyes over me from head to toe. "It's supposed to. Pain can be pleasurable though…"

Oh God, he said that. He went there first and my mind followed.

I sucked in a breath and rolled my eyes flinching when he dug his fingertips in verging on painful. "Sure, it *can be*… but it's not right now."

He let out a long breath when I sighed, the muscles in his arms tensing and the heat in his hands seemed to feel like fire on my skin.

He looked down at me, giving me this scorching gaze and I understood right then why women would fall for him despite the attitude. It was that stare that got them. I was sure of it. His eyes were so intense, bright green, hands splayed over me. There was just something about the way they held you in place like the sun when you stared at it. Yeah, the harshness, the brightness burned but once your eyes drifted that way, there was no way you could look away. When you blinked, finally relieving the burn, you still saw that same bright image behind your lids because it was there, reminding you of the intensity.

I blinked slowly looking up at him, my eyes wide, my breath shallow.

Destry seemed to be having the same reaction when I felt both hands move higher. His tongue slid over his lower lip and he leaned forward, hunched over my leg slightly.

Look at that tongue. And look at the way that body curves around. Imagine that hovering over your entire body!

I'd give anything to know what he was thinking right now. Why was he looking at me like this?

He blinked, slowly, his hands moved higher and settled at my knee, then worked back down the outsides of my leg. When he spoke, I could feel his warm breath wash over me. "The muscle is tense. You should ice it tonight. It'll keep it from cramping up."

I bit my lip to keep from gasping when he didn't let up, and then increased the pressure slightly. I flinched and jerked my leg back.

His eyes hardened, his voice low. "Did that hurt?"

The pain from his grip was worth it. I wanted his hands all over me. *Pull my hair too. Go ahead. Pull my fucking hair and spank me!*

"A little." I glanced up but I couldn't stay focused on him. No way. My other leg fell open slightly and left me basically spread eagle before him on the floor.

Destry glanced away, a low rumble in his chest as his jaw clenched, his warm fingers moving even higher above my knee though his words were a goodbye. "Okay... well, I'll see you Thursday. Ice that leg and get plenty of water and rest."

What was that? Was he turned on?

You definitely wouldn't know it judging by the impassive expression he wore.

He flattened his palms on my leg, dragged them slowly down until he reached my ankle and then pulled away, his breathing a little heavier than before. He looked like he wanted to say something as he placed my foot back down on the mat, his elbows resting on his knees, but he didn't. Instead he shifted his hips as if he was uncomfortable.

We stared at each other, neither one of us moving.

He quirked an eyebrow at me, curiously, then reached for his sweatshirt beside him and put it in his lap, shielding my view of his hips.

He wanted to stand up but he was hesitating and I think I knew why. He was aroused too. Internally I was jumping for joy. He had to put his sweatshirt in his lap. That meant something, right?

I watched him walk away, when his body was turned the other way, he raised the sweatshirt and slung it over his shoulder. He was definitely hiding something.

A little dumbfounded, I stared at the ring shaking my head as he disappeared. Flopping back against the mat I ran my hands over my face.

You're in deep, Tallan. Deep.

I couldn't stay on the mat, or here, since I had dinner plans. As I was gathering my sweatshirt and shoes, I wanted to change into jeans since I was meeting Jared and Catie for dinner at the Crab Pot tonight. I didn't exactly want to change in the middle of the basement, or in that horrific bathroom, but I remembered Destry saying there was a locker room. What I thought was a back exit was a small hallway that led to what was surely a locker room. Inside was a charcoal wall with about six black metal lockers, two wooden benches and what looked to be two showers lined with dark gray tile. It wasn't exactly the cleanest of locker rooms but you could tell it was used regularly and in much better shape than the one by the stairs.

On the bench was Destry's sweatshirt he wore on our run and his black shorts and white Nike shoes. Which meant he was in here.

Walk out right now. What if he's naked?

All the more reason to stay.

I peeked around the corner to see if he was in the bathroom.

There was no one in sight but I did hear the shower turn on and nearly pissed my pants when a naked, completely naked, Destry stepped inside the shower. He must have been standing on the other side of the wall and hadn't heard me come in. *Sweet Jesus, look at his body.*

My eyes frantically swept over his entire body, memorizing every inch knowing any second I would leave here and never get to see something this perfectly toned and delicious again. I've seen recent pictures of Silas and he had nothing on Destry's body. Everywhere I looked muscles bulged and skin seemed tight. Unlike Silas, Destry didn't have any tattoos, which seemed rare these days. Even I had tattoos. But if my body looked like that, I'm not sure I'd mar it with ink either. His entire body was a work of art, he didn't need anything else to make him hotter.

I forced my eyes up to his face, cursing the half wall blocking his lower half from the lower waist down.

All I could think about was, strip your clothes away and shower with him. There was no way he'd allow that. Knowing him, he'd humiliate me even more so staying out here was better.

I almost left. Almost.

That was until he ducked his shoulder, adjusting the water and I saw his bare ass. I might as well have gotten popcorn at that point because there was no fucking way I was leaving this show now.

The first few minutes of the shower were boring as he washed away sweat, his hair, face. And then the moment of truth...his hands traveled lower and I knew damn well what those hands were touching.

I felt dirty. Scandalous. And guess what? I didn't care. Not at all. My breathing slowed and became ragged. I was a voyeur, a sweaty voyeur who needed and wanted to watch everything he was doing.

I knew he was doing something with those hands, he had to have been by the way his head fell forward. He moved and leaned back against the wall of the shower.

If only I was taller! Damn it, where's my high heels when I really need them?

There's a stool in the basement. *Would it be weird if I got it and then came back in here?*

Don't do that. He could be done by then.

I didn't. But I wanted to.

Destry let out a heavy breath, his eyes drifting closed as he shifted again and pressed his back into the wall. *Fantastic!* Finally a view I could work with. My eyes traveled down that gorgeous body and lower to where his hands were.

Destry.

Was.

Touching.

Himself.

The sight before me made my mouth go dry. It was like his stare. A vision forever burned in my memory. Words couldn't do that sight justice and the blazing heat shot through my body when I saw his hand move and stroke over possibly the best looking dick I've ever seen. I've seen four but still, he could have been a cock model. And he was shaved, which made me want to run over there and touch the smooth skin over his balls.

What the fuck has happened to me? Was I denied oxygen for too long during that run? Was the lack of calorie intake causing me to openly gawk at him pleasuring himself? Who is this person in this body of mine?

Standing there, I pressed my thighs together like I was about to wet myself but really I just needed some pressure, friction, anything. Something. My entire body shook as I tried to stay still and not fall on the floor. I even had to put my hand against the wall to hold myself up. My fucking knees were going weak.

In that moment I would have done anything for him. He needed a mouth on that dick. Fuck the hand. He needed my mouth!

Look at that man. Toned muscles, hard and perfect all over. What the fuck was Stella thinking?

Goddamn. It was just sinful to look that good.

When he started to stroke himself with some determination, his head leaned back against the tile, eyes closed, I was both captivated and feeling a little like I shouldn't be watching. But this porn show was too good to pass up. Voyeur, party of one.

This was most certainly a total invasion of privacy but I chalked it up for research for the article. Character development. If I was going to write about him, I needed personal details. At least that was what I was trying to convince myself of.

Oh come on, Tallan. You're not writing a fucking novel. You're writing a sports article.

"Shut up." I told myself watching his powerful hand give himself pleasure I so desperately wanted to help him out with. I had a good look at his entire body now and it was flawless. So fucking flawless I wanted to run my tongue over every smooth surface and suck on him.

Oh yeah, most definitely deprived of oxygen.

Let's be honest though, no woman in their right mind would turn away from watching this. They'd be crazy if they did.

For at least ten minutes, I watched him stroke himself. He had some fucking endurance that's for sure. Imagine how long he could go. And believe me, I was in awe of his ability to drag this out. I was read to come myself at minute two just watching him.

Look at him. *Just look at him.*

My eyes burned around the steam from the shower and I tried to keep them open. That's when I realized what was happening. He was about to come and my panties were soaked.

Destry's feet braced wider, his strong body hunched over slightly as his knees bent. His left hand gripped his dick harder, moving vigorously now, the other splayed out against the tile wall. His muscles in his chest tensed, his head bent forward as his hand moves faster between his legs.

He didn't make any audible sound but just a moment later and he came on his hand and stomach. It was unbelievably hot. That was the single most powerful sexy few minutes of my entire life.

My hand covered my mouth when I saw that white liquid cover his hand at what I just witnessed.

Was he thinking of me?

My mind desperately wanted that.

I could barely remain standing after that. My face pressed against the concrete wall when Destry moved under the spray, water beading off his body.

I felt like I'd just watched a porno. A good one too. I wanted to run in there, straddle him, and dry hump the guy. And then beg him to fuck me.

That's the day my pussy wanted to be friends with Destry. Good friends. She didn't care if he was a dick. Even better if he was. That way she wouldn't have some sort of silly attachment to him. This way I could get some action, yet still get prepared for Silas.

Shit. Look at me making a plan. A fucked up plan. I couldn't focus after that. All I thought about was Destry in the shower.

I wasn't sure how I would ever face him again let alone not imagine what I saw every time I heard his name.

As quietly as I could I backed out of the locker room, changed into my jeans, wished I had spare panties and walked across the street to the Crab Pot.

Jared and Catie were already seated near the window overlooking the pier when I got over there. My appearance was noticeably flushed.

"Rough day at the gym?"

I waved my hand around trying to blow it off. "We went for a run and I couldn't breathe."

"That's not from a run, told you she was macking on Destry." Jared burst out laughing nudging Catie's shoulder with his own. "She looks like she just got caught with her hand in the cookie jar."

Oh my God, if they only knew where a hand was five minutes ago and what I'd just been watching. I still had the after effects of my unsatisfied arousal on my mind and blushed like I was twelve. So busted. This made them both laugh even harder. Catie even joined in. Where was the girl's alliance to her bestie?

"Seriously, guys, he's a dick. He hates me, I hate him, it's a mutually beneficial relationship."

"But you are going to still write that article for Marcus on him, right?" Jared inquired.

"I don't honestly know how I can do it. He refuses to discuss anything that doesn't have to do with burning calories and getting fit." Burning calories, yep, my mind went there again.

"How about I see if I can find any dirt on him by seeing if he has an arrest record, that could be a start?" Jared mentions this while shoving some of the most amazing calamari strips into his mouth as he patted his stomach and grinned the biggest grin I'd ever seen from him.

"Fucking brilliant idea, Jared, and while you are at it, fuck you and that calamari you just inhaled and your abs." Jared knew exactly what he was doing, the asshole.

He almost choked with laughter. *Yeah, choke on that squid you pig!*

Well, an arrest record, if there was one, was at least a start on getting some personal information on Destry. Yeah, I could write this article, I loved research after all and that's all any good article was about. I'd get the dirt on Destry without his input. Research and interviews, my stomping grounds.

"Do it, Jared, I've got to have something to go on because he's not spilling a thing."

Oh. My. God. Did I just say he's not spilling a thing when what I saw him just spill in that shower had me squirming in this seat, in front of my friends.

Jared smirked, like he knew exactly what I'd just witnessed. That motherfucker better not say a damn thing to me.

"Let's order some food." Quick change of subject, party of one?

I sighed, well, almost cried, as I ordered a glass of water, salad with dressing on the side and blackened salmon plain. All the while Jared shoveled a few more pieces of calamari in his mouth and ordered an appetizer of crab cakes. God I hated him right now, absolutely hated him. Catie was no better, she was right along with him eating crab by the pound, which I stole a few bites of. I need to seriously rethink the alliances I make in this world, or at least the restaurant choices they make.

Tuesday
April 12, 2011

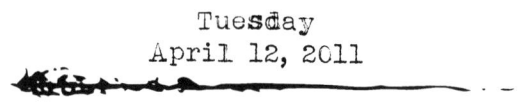

Tuesday morning, I got onto my laptop and did some research on Destry. After I stalked Silas' Twitter feed. Nothing had been posted other than a picture of him performing in Atlanta. I felt a little weird, here I was stalking Silas, but I could not get those images of Destry out of my head. In fact, they were on repeat. Sexy slide show.

Google was helpful and gave me all the details on James and Denise, Destry's parents. Unfortunately it didn't give me a lot on Stella Summers. I knew it had to do with her, especially knowing she left him after that fight. He had a right to be bitter. No guy is that bitter without a woman fucking them over. I've learned that from my ex-boss. She fucked so many guys over that she had her own hate page on the internet. I added fuel to that shit as often as I could. Posted once a month on my behalf.

Jared came home around noon, pleasantly happy the door was locked, holding a folder of what appeared to be Destry's arrest record. And it was thick. Mostly minor shit like disturbing the peace, vandalism, but then there was a vehicle theft.

80

"It was his car so technically he didn't steal it." Jared said, shrugging, his hands hanging on his bullet proof vest. "He was just taking it back, apparently, but she called the police on him anyways."

"Who took it back?"

"His ex, Stella Summers."

"Oh." I looked through the rest of the folder and then to Jared. "Isn't this illegal for me to have this?"

"Don't tell anyone where you got it from and we're good." Then he smiled heading for the door. "I should have been a fucking detective."

"Don't get ahead of yourself." And then I remembered it was Tuesday. "Tacos tonight?"

"Yeah." Jared nodded walking backwards. "I'm off at five."

"Okay."

I had been good all week. I was having tacos tonight.

When Jared left, I got on YouTube and decided it was time to watch this boy fight. I got out my notepad and typed in "Stone vs. Lucas." Hundreds of videos popped up.

I clicked on the one titled: Knock out that was five minutes long.

They actually started that video with the introductions. The whole production of a fight, which I had never been to, was unreal. It was like a rock concert.

"Here is your heavyweight champion of the world, *Destry Stone!*" Then Destry appeared from the shadows, stone faced and silent as he made the slow walk toward the ring while Linkin Park's "Wretches and Kings" blared.

They went through all the introductions, said those famous words I knew, "Let's get ready to rumble!"

Various lines in the commentary caught my attention.

"He's in the best physical and mental state he's ever been. This is just an upset for everyone."

As the fight progressed, round after round, it looked like Destry had the upper hand.

"He's good at keeping his distance and he doesn't move back into the ropes, he moves around his opponent. Lucas can't stand directly in front of Stone that way. It's disaster. He's not feeling him out at all. He's just positioning himself in front of him, flat footed. He's not moving and Stone sees that. It's only a matter of time before he finds the right combination and ends the fight."

Then round five comes and Destry was a different fighter all together. His attention was on the crowd, more importantly on Stella who was seated to his right. Every few seconds, he'd glance at her. And then he just stood there. Kept backing away and ending up in the ropes. Lucas had him in the ropes, delivering jab after jab when he came back with a left hook, and a blow to the side of his head. Destry went down. He didn't even try to get up.

"It's over. We have a brand new heavyweight champion of the world!"

The camera spun to Destry, now standing in the corner with his trainer, only his eyes weren't on the belt being handed to the new WBC champion of the world. It was on his girl walking out on him.

I sat there staring at the screen that I'd paused on Destry's face. No wonder the guys such a dick to everyone. I Googled "Destry Stone and Stella Summers" to see what came up.

It was image after image of them together at various events, in Seattle, on vacation, you name it, for two years. It was clear he adored her with the look on his face in every photograph. That my friends was a man in love. No doubt. The man in those photographs was very different from the man I saw five days a week.

I had to leave for a couple hours to pick up my dry cleaning and then get my nails done. By the time I got back Jared was home and the comforting smell of flank steak tacos was filling the hallways.

When I got inside our apartment and set my bags down, I looked around expecting Catie to be here. "Where's Catie?"

Jared didn't look up from his chopping as he prepared his salsa. "Home, I guess."

"You didn't invite her?"

"Why would I? Taco Tuesday is our thing."

I smiled, liking that Jared and I had a thing. No matter how close

I felt to Catie because she was the only girlfriend I tolerated, it would never compare to the comfort I felt around Jared. There's nothing I couldn't tell him. Sometimes he made fun of me, but then there were times where he gave me exactly what I needed to hear. A man's unbiased point of view.

He knew something was up with me immediately. "What's wrong? You've been acting weird since the Crab Pot."

I shrugged trying to distract him with the new chips I picked up to go with the salsa. "These are made fresh every day."

He reached forward and grabbed the bag. "Are you mad Catie was at lunch with us yesterday?"

He was so far off the mark that I had to set up straight now. With a deep inhale, I blurted it out. "I saw Destry jacking off in the shower yesterday."

He stopped chopping, maybe even stopped breathing. His reaction was somewhat entertaining. Jared wasn't sure what to make of that. You wouldn't know he was going to say anything by his impassive stare, but then a smile quirked his lips. "Why were you watching?"

"I didn't mean to." I braced my hands on the counter and leaned in. "I needed to change, he was in there, I stayed and watched. Now I feel guilty."

"You should feel guilty. We do that shit in private."

I laughed when he said "we" because I knew damn well Jared still jerked off. He may be twenty-three but he still indulged in the self-pleasure. No man spends forty-five minutes in the shower without doing that.

"You're missing the point."

Jared was quiet, his eyes dropped from mine to the cutting board. "Have you caught me?"

"No," I laughed.

"Good."

"Well, not this week." A huge grin spread over my face.

He threw some cilantro at me.

I sighed, dramatically. "Should I say anything to him?"

"No." Jared shook his head immediately. "Don't. Just pretend you didn't see anything."

"I'm not sure I can look at him again. It was the hottest thing I've ever seen. I mean, that was…" I felt my cheeks flush remembering the way his body bent over when he came. "It was sexy."

"I don't think I need to hear this. I want to enjoy my tacos and not think of a guy beating off in the shower."

"Oh come on, you said you wanted to know what was wrong. So I told you."

"No, I asked you if it was because of Catie. If I would have known it had to do with Destry, and him in the shower, I wouldn't have asked."

Our conversation slowed as we prepared dinner but when we sat down at the table, I had to ask, "So what's really with you and Catie?"

Jared brought random girls home every once in a while but for the last six months, it had only been Catie.

"We're just having sex, Tallan." He took a bit of his taco, chewing slowly, and then added, "There's nothing to it."

I took a chip and loaded it with salsa. "So you don't love her?" I then shoved the chip in my mouth.

"No," he seemed annoyed that I was asking. "Not in that way."

"And how does she feel?"

"We haven't talked about it. I think she's sleeping with a guy she works with too."

"Oh." My eyes dropped from his face to my taco I hadn't touched yet, instead I'd been feasting on chips.

Jared shrugged, took a drink of his beer and then rested his elbows on the table preparing to eat his second taco. "We've never said we were exclusive so I can't be too bent."

"But you want to be… exclusive?"

"I don't even know anymore. I'm just focused on getting this probation year over with and then I guess I'll see what happens."

The look he gave me told me he had feelings for Catie. He just wasn't sure what they meant.

I could definitely relate to him.

Thursday
April 14, 2011

When I got to the bar that night and down to the basement, Destry was in the ring with another guy sparring. Danny was standing near the weights, his arms crossed over his black t-shirt that read *Danny's* on the back.

I looked at Danny, standing next to him. If anyone would give me the real scoop on Destry Stone, it would be his uncle, right?

When he noticed me, he smiled slightly.

"What's his deal?"

The hint of a smile he had dropped. I don't think Danny wanted to answer me truthfully. But he did answer. "He's angry."

Angry was an understatement for Destry. Just watching him now, it was apparent.

"Has he always been this way?"

Danny contemplated answering me, again, and then said, "No. He hasn't. He was a happy kid, for a while and then life happened and it knocked him down. He always found a way to win. An advantage. But he couldn't that night." Danny's voice had a distance to it that I didn't quite understand. Almost like he was talking about someone who had died. In a way, a part of Destry did die that night. You could easily see that watching the video of that fight.

The commotion in the ring caught my attention.

The way he jabbed at the guy I couldn't keep up with how fast he was. The power, the determination, the skill, it was all impressive to me, and unbelievably hot. He was quick, his foot work and the way he bounced on the balls of his feet as he paced his sparring partner was impeccable just like the quickness behind his powerful hits. I was in awe at his ability, strength and control in the ring. I knew then there was no way he lost that fight. No fucking way a guy like him wasn't ready.

I felt bad for his sparring partner. He couldn't see the punches coming at him let alone defend himself against them. Destry then delivered another, then a body shot and a right jab.

The guy bowed out after that and waved his arm at Destry. "I'm done, Destry."

Destry nodded, held his gloved hands up and spit his mouth guard out. He turned and saw me standing there for the first time and our eyes locked. Usually Destry doesn't look at me long. There were fleeting glances, but for some reason he stared at me right then and I was trapped, unable to lift my gaze from his.

Immediately his naked body was in my mind and gone was that white t-shirt he was wearing right now and those black shorts all but evaporated. All I saw in that moment was him naked in the shower.

Forever burned into my memory.

His trainer approached him, giving him feedback, showing him video footage on his phone of the sparring sessions and then dropping his shoulder to give him an example. It was interesting to me to watch the way Destry was intently listening to him. I wouldn't think he would listen to anyone.

I learned a lot about him when he wasn't looking or when he was interacting with others. He's quietly confident and has a sense of arrogance, yes, but it's not displayed in the ways you would think. He's a totally different person around me so seeing this side of him had me captivated.

When his trainer left, Destry approached me as I sat on the mats stretching out my legs. My calf was still sore but it wasn't as bad as before. He was right, ice helped.

"Let's start with a run." His foot lightly kicked at my thigh as his hand reached out to help me up. His left hand. The one that two nights ago was touching his dick.

Take that hand, Tallan. Lick it!

"You're gonna do two full miles today."

Sometimes I'm not sure whether I should be afraid of Destry, or simply laugh at him. Was he crazy?

Reaching up I pushed my hair out of my eyes. "The fuck you say."

Neither one of us broke eye contact because I could be a shit head too. He's met his equal when it comes to shitheads and I think, no, I know by the way he was staring at me he realized it right then. "Okay…" he paused and leaned into the wall, his head bent forward but his eyes rose to meet mine. "Cardio gives you… endurance. Think of it that way. You want endurance, don't you?"

Goddamn him. He was doing this on purpose. I knew it.

We went for a run. And amazingly, I went the full two miles. Just one week ago you couldn't get me to run a block, now look at me. I blamed, or should I thank Destry for that. I was always running to keep up with him because there was no way I would let him run behind me and see the very thing I was here to rid myself of.

Two fucking miles. Might as well have been two hundred because I wanted to die when I was done and contemplated having Mr. Gravity help me out again by rolling down the stairs to the basement. Instead I just held onto the handrail and prayed to the gods with each downward step. Back in the basement, I laid on the mats, face first panting and holding my calf. It still hurt only now it was cramping up.

"Do you want me to massage it again?"

Fuck yes, I do.

"No." I turned over and flopped myself on my back. "That's okay."

"Take a bath in ice." I peeked one eye open when he spoke. His stare was unnerving. "It helps."

He was quiet for a moment as I sat up and watched him as he leaned into the wall.

"I don't have a bathtub. Only a shower."

Destry pushed himself away from the wall and closed the distance between us. "You can use my place."

"The locker room?" My eyes betrayed me. They went to his crotch.

"No, my apartment. I have a bathtub." When I didn't say anything, his mouth twitched running his hand over his jaw. "Is that a yes?"

The words came out before I could stop them. "Yes."

I'm not sure what I expected when I thought about Destry's apartment, but I didn't expect this. There was absolutely nothing in the way of photographs or decorations. It was nice with black stone tile in the entry way and kitchen that met dark wood floors in the living room. Against the wall in the living room was a brown leather couch, a rather nice one that appeared to be slept on quite often. Surrounding it was about a dozen empty beer bottles and one empty vodka bottle. In the corner next to a window that overlooked the city was a punching bag hung from the ceiling. Against the opposite wall from the couch was a television mounted on the wall.

That was it.

As I walked further into his apartment, I gathered he was a necessities only type of guy but had expensive taste.

"You want some water?" Destry asked from behind. "Or a beer."

I turned around to look at him. "Yes, water please."

He moved around me to the stainless steel fridge and retrieved two bottles of water and handed me one. I got a peek in his fridge and it was a lot like his house. Empty.

I got the cap off and took a drink. I loved cold water, it was so refreshing. But it also might have something to do with me needing something to occupy myself because Destry was without a shirt now.

I told myself not to look. I did repeatedly. But none of that shit worked.

Then again, I didn't want to appear too obvious so I did that trick where I held the water bottle out in front of me and zoned past it.

Destry caught on because who the hell really looks at a water bottle?

Well, I would, but this time I wasn't.

What did he do?

Destry isn't the type of guy to pop off with a cheesy line or even say anything for that matter. There was a small hint of a smile, but nothing notable. He watched me, let his eyes drift south to the curves of my body. Then he raised his arm and pointed behind me. "Bathroom's that way. Towels are under the sink."

I couldn't stay there staring at him so I took off down the hall which wasn't a hall at all. It was like a cutout in the living room, two doors. A bedroom and a bathroom.

After closing the door behind me, I set my water on the counter and stared at myself in the mirror. I looked like crap. My face was all flushed, hair matted and tossed up into a messy ponytail. As I stared at myself, I was both concerned but strangely satisfied that my arms and stomach already felt a little tighter. It's only been two weeks. Was that even possible?

Well, with Destry, it seemed that way. Look at his body.

I'd just gotten my clothes off and bath running when I decided to snoop through his medicine cabinet.

Seemed appropriate. Who wouldn't go through a man's medicine cabinet? All in the name of research.

I bet Stella did. I stood there for a brief moment, my bare feet on cold tile while I decided if going through his personal belongings was an invasion of privacy. It most certainly was but I'd already crossed the privacy line when I so openly watched him in the shower.

I was a little nervous but when I opened it, there was barely anything in there but tooth paste, a toothbrush, contact lens cleaner, deodorant, clippers and what looked to be a prescription. I picked the bottle up and read the label.

Vicodin.
Destry J. Stone
Take every 4-6 hours as needed for pain.

Hmm. Interesting.

He didn't have much to look at so I decided to get in the tub. It felt so strange to be in some man's apartment, naked, in his tub. Like I couldn't relax enough to enjoy it.

Just when I started to relax slightly, Destry walked in, still with no shirt on and carrying a bucket.

"Destry, oh my God!" I tried to cover myself but really, he saw it all before I had time. And he looked. Bluntly. Like he'd planned that.

"Ice water is best for sore muscles."

"Are you shitting me right now? I'm naked."

He shrugged and dumped the bucket in my bath. "So what? You saw me naked on Monday, in the shower, yes?"

Oh my fuck! He knew I was watching him!

My mouth gaped open, not only from that damn ice but also that I was caught. How embarrassing. I could feel the rush of warmth to my cheeks. And elsewhere. Destry had that presence about him.

I thought maybe he would dump the ice in and then leave. Walks away a lot. But no, the fucker sat down on the toilet beside the tub.

"Are you for real?" I cupped my boobs with my palms and crossed my legs. "What are you doing?"

He tapped the side of the tub with his index finger. "You said your leg was hurting. Let me see it."

"What? No. Get out."

"Oh come on, I'm not looking." He laughed, actually laughed. Slowly he lowered his gaze and stared at my stomach and hips. "Okay, well now I am, but let me see your leg." There's a certain amount of authority in his voice that I couldn't ignore.

I tried though. "No."

"It's only fair, Tallan. Don't you think?"

I didn't say anything. My body was literally shaking again. He'd caught me watching him and he didn't say anything? Who does that?

"Nothing to say?" He asked.

When I was about to scream, he picked up the bucket and dropped the ice cubes in the tub and smiled.

"What?" I jumped at the shock of the ice. "No. I'm sorry."

"Don't be. I hope you enjoyed the view." His eyes crinkled at the corners when he grinned. "Care to give me a view now?"

"Are you serious? I can't tell with you?"

His hand reached inside the ice water and retrieved a handful of ice. "I don't joke around often. So what do you think?"

Taking it in the palm of his hand, he then placed it over my calf. I shivered, but not from the ice when he trailed a finger down my left leg. Destry was touching my bare leg. And he was massaging my leg. Again.

Would it be weird if I grabbed his hand and shoved it between my legs?

Yeah, don't do that. You'll scare him away.

I closed my eyes as he massaged my leg. I ached to be touched higher. I wanted him to touch me there. I wanted good sex. I wanted it so bad it was becoming all I thought about. I felt like a teenage boy. The thing was, a week ago I wanted that with Silas and I was ready to jump at the opportunity. Now, well my pussy had made a friend and she wanted a play date.

I felt like I needed to brace myself, so I did. I moved my hands to the edge of the tub.

That left me bare and exposed from the waist up.

Destry, meet my boobs. Give them a tit shake if you'd like.

He let out a long breath and unconsciously, it seemed, moved his hand higher than necessary.

"You can go higher." I said, swallowing the lump in my throat from the nerves and the increasing throbbing pleasure his touch was causing me.

His eyes flickered to mine, dark and stayed on mine. "If I do... I won't stop."

"Then don't stop."

His chest was heaving and he eyed me, and then scooted back about a foot from me. He ran his hands through his hair making it stand up on end. Then he stood wiping his hands on the towel on the counter. With his eyes on mine, he reached inside his shorts and adjusted himself. In front of me.

Sweet. Fucking. Jesus.

He winked when I noticed. "Hungry?"

"I... uh... what?"

"For food." He laughed quietly, amused with himself. "Are you hungry for food?"

I made this squeak sound when I sighed sinking down in the tub. "Yes. Since I met you I'm always hungry. Food would be good."

What was I doing? I hired a guy to get me into shape and here I am two weeks into it and I'm writing an article about him, watching him naked in the shower and now letting him watch me naked, massage my leg with ice cubes, and telling him to touch me higher.

What the fuck?

Chapter Seven
KISSED THE CANVAS

When a boxer is knocked down face first on to the canvas. In the old days they would say his face was in the resin of the canvas.

Monday
April 18, 2011

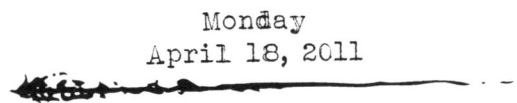

That night in his apartment after I got out of the tub, we sat around his living room eating carb filled Chinese food. As weird as it sounded, I felt like it was changing the dynamic of our relationship.

Everything he said made me wonder what the fuck he was talking about. I would latch onto certain words and then spend the entire night trying to decipher them and they're meaning. Annoyed the hell out of me. I would wonder if they were meant for me or if they were about someone else.

The thing was, the more time I spent around him, the more research I did, the more I wanted to help him. The more I wanted to know about him.

Then I hated him more because he was invading my brain. I didn't want to think about him like this. My goal here was Silas, my ex who I was trying to get back.

Why was he even affecting me at all?

Why did I care if he was nice or not?

I was a woman on a mission.

I shouldn't want the answer. I shouldn't care at all. He was just a personal trainer and this was the article. I blamed Marcus. I blamed Jared. Really anyone but myself at that point.

You know when I started caring was when Marcus put the story in my head and made me believe I could make a difference in Destry's life. I could change the public perception of what they perceived as Destry lost the fight or threw the fight. For once someone could make a difference for him instead of using him. It was when Marcus presented the idea that I *had* to get to know him. I was researching him and then I was convinced that there was so much more to the man behind the harsh image that he so desperately wanted people to believe was really him. When it wasn't at all. There was a side with so much passion that it was damn near blinding to be around him. It was almost as if nothing you did or said was as good as what he could be, if he let himself. He was most definitely holding back.

It was nearing seven Monday night when I got to the bar. Destry wasn't down there yet so I waited for him when my phone rang. The number wasn't one I recognized but maybe it was Destry calling. "Hello?"

"Hey, Tallan." A man's voice rang through, one that I recognized but couldn't place.

"Hey?" I said, a little unsure and then it dawned on me that it was Silas. My heart started pounding in my chest. "Silas?"

"Yeah, it's me. So… still on for the concert in a few weeks?" His words seemed rushed, commotion all around him. "I'm back in the states now but I just wanted to check."

I laughed lightly, then noticed Destry approach carrying his bag and a sweatshirt. Immediately I wanted off the phone. I didn't want Destry to see me so vulnerable and Silas caused that. Destry had shown me in the past few weeks how strong I could be and having him witness this conversation wiped all that to shit.

Destry stopped and leaned into the brick wall staring at his phone. "Did you think I forgot?"

"No." Silas said, his breathing and words evening out. "But I was worried that maybe you would call it off. It's a lot for me to ask and I don't deserve it. I could understand if you didn't want to see me again after what went down after high school."

Ya think?

I didn't say anything in response because, in reality, there's some truth to that. I was also so damn nervous with Destry standing this close. Anything I said he could hear and would most certainly judge me without saying a word, the look he'd give me would be humiliating enough.

"But I want to see you."

I sighed, turning my body away from Destry and into the wall. "Why?"

Noticing I was attempting to gain some privacy, he shrugged and tossed his bag to the ground. He didn't care who I was talking to.

"I'm just going through some shit and it'd be a nice to hang with a familiar face."

"Of course, I can't wait to see you and catch up." Speaking in such low tones, I'm not entirely sure he even heard me with all of the commotion and background noise on his end but Destry certainly heard. It was so quiet in here I might has well have been moaning like a whore in church talking to him.

Right then I felt bad for Silas, mostly because I couldn't imagine the lifestyle he now had. Different city every night and your closest family and friends never by your side. You can only live that life for so long. Deep down he had to have known the lifestyle he chose would result in isolation. It always does.

Silas said he'd call in a week or so and make sure I got the ticket.

When I hung up, Destry dropped his bag from his shoulder and looked up at me. "I'm curious, what do you see in that guy?"

"What guy?" I shrugged. He was so good at it I figured I would try my hand at it now.

He almost seemed amused at my response. Almost. He was still waiting for an answer and I was beginning to understand when Destry wanted an answer, he got one.

"You mean Silas Cade?" I put my hands on my hips.

Destry's eyes traveled south taking in my body. I pulled at my dark gray t-shirt trying to make sure it wasn't clinging to my body. When I thought about it, Destry made no attempt to hide his attraction today or any other day based on the usual once over he always managed to give me. Attraction. Or maybe he wasn't even attracted to me. Maybe he was horny. I watched his eyes, staring at my lips. Yeah, that was it.

The thing was, I didn't miss the fact that he was looking at least. I blushed, to which he winked.

Oh my God, was he flirting?

No way. Guys like Destry don't flirt. They don't need to.

But then he spoke and I wanted to punch him because his mouth ruined everything.

"You're stupid for going. I can tell you that right now. He's not looking to talk."

Back to douche mode.

"You don't know a damn thing about Silas." I said defensively, starting to get pissed at everyone and their comments. Did they really think I was that dumb? "So what if he wants me. Who are you to fucking judge me for that? Not everyone fucks around with every girl who spreads her goddamn legs. Maybe I want that for once." I resaid my statement in my head and realized it didn't make a lot of sense.

"Not everyone fucks around with every girl that spreads her goddamn legs."

What?

It was his turn to get defensive, and he did. "Are you saying that's me?" He stepped forward, kind of like he did with Stella when she challenged him.

"Sure looks that way given the girl who walked in here the other day." I backed up to create distance between us, my back pressing into the cool brick wall.

"Who are you to fucking judge me?" He stepped back and raised his hands. "I had one girlfriend. *One.* I was with her for two goddamn years. I've fucked five girls my entire life. Five." He shook his head, anger evident in the stare that pinned me to the wall, made me feel guilty for assuming. "Fuck you for thinking otherwise."

Not only did I strike a nerve, but it wasn't lost on me that Destry was a good guy and all this time I'd been thinking he was some kind of man whore. Never assume apparently.

I suppose he had every right to be pissed off, but so did I.

"I'm sorry. I'm just tired of everyone judging me. I want to do this and I don't want to be talked out of it." I looked down at my hands, and then at Destry.

He didn't say anything for a few minutes, just stared down at me. He was literally driving me mad. I wanted to know what he was thinking right then so freaking bad. There was a thick silence between us, almost awkward and standing that close to him made me anxious, nervous even.

"Fair enough." He winked, though it seemed forced, and motioned toward the weights, his body relaxing but still tense. "Let's start with lunges."

Lunges weren't my favorite and he knew it. He was punishing me.

After lunges we did fucking sixty second planks. Who the hell dreams up this shit? We did full on planks, side planks, and if Destry could have figured out a way, I'm sure he would have made me twist into a pretzel to do planks.

He corrected my form many times, had to touch me every time, in every place to make sure my plank form was straight as the proverbial plank would be. He watched me jump rope and then sat behind me counting as I did squats with a bar.

I did the same circuit type training as last week when he was showing me some squats. Apparently my form was off. "You're still not doing it right," he said, standing up.

Nudging my thighs apart with his hips pressed forward so he was right against my ass, I sighed. Openly sighed. I couldn't take much more of this touching with him. He'd been doing it all day. It was so different from every other day. Normally he kept his distance and now look at him, touching, showing, interacting. Not when I was so frustrated, stressed out, and horny.

His face was near my ear as he said, "Good form is as important as exercise and hydration. Bend your knees and keep breathing."

I did and then it happened. My ass slid down his dick. Slid all down that, all in his business.

And. AND. He was hard.

I turned my head immediately and stared at him.

He winked.

The way that wink made me feel right then should have been illegal. He wasn't supposed to be making me feel these things right now. He was a trainer. I was a girl looking to get in shape and meeting my long lost love in a few weeks. I didn't need to be getting turned on by winks, his smart ass remarks, and his hard on. I needed to hate him.

Destry tensed behind me when my back arched on instinct. Give me a hard dick and I'm gonna treat it like a stripper pole all greased up and ready just for me. I basically grinded into his dick. No shame in my game at all. His hands flew to my hips, his lips at my ear. "Wanna get a drink with me?"

"With you?" I asked, turning around to face him. "Like right now?"

He looked down, his eyes on my lips, then searching my eyes and breathing heavy. "Yes. With me. We're done for the day."

I swallowed, as if I hadn't drank water in days and Destry was like a desert mirage I needed to get to and taste. "Okay…"

I think there's a point in your life when you know something is changing. You feel it when the decision is made. That was right then for me. Torn between all the reasons that had brought me to Destry, I was at a crossroads.

Silas. Destry.

Destry was here, now. Silas was a rock star who, for all I knew wanted me for just one night and then would leave me just like he did after high school, to pursue his dreams that didn't include me. How had this man standing before me caused me to doubt the very thing I was working so hard for?

But I knew what that one drink meant. With me, it was the point of no return. Decisions made with the assistance of liquid courage were never a good idea.

"How'd you meet him?"

I laughed as Destry and I sat at the bar together. It was a Monday night, a handful of bar patrons filled the tables all watching the Mariners game. And here he was, asking questions about Silas again. "I thought you didn't care?"

His turn to laugh. His fingers wrapped around the glass as he stared at the contents. "Well no, I don't. But I'm just trying to understand why a girl like you would be doing all this for him. I'm curious. So how'd you meet him?"

"Well, you have to realize that I was thirteen when I met Silas. And we were inseparable. Then one day he left, with no explanation at all. When I got to college I met friends, moved on in a way but no one ever came close to the way I felt about him. That's why I want to see him again. Just one night."

Destry didn't say anything but handed me a shot of vodka and then downed his own, as if he knew the pain I felt. "And what happens if that night doesn't go as planned?"

"I haven't thought about that part yet." The thing was, I was refusing to let myself think about that part of it.

He nodded, his eyes on his shot glass again.

"You know that old saying, something about the best laid plans often go awry. You should really think about the what ifs before you show up to meet him." Destry wouldn't make eye contact when he said that. "Celebrities are no different than professional athletes, opportunities are presented to you that are oftentimes hard to pass up when you are in the public eye."

Damn him. Silas wasn't like that, surely he wasn't. Was he?

We ended up making small talk for a while, but with Destry there were some topics that were off limits. It seemed anything related to his past, his family, and a lot about boxing were all triggers. It was certainly hard to have conversations with him. You could literally watch him shut down when the conversation drifted towards an outcome he couldn't control.

"I'm so out of practice." I said randomly, as if he should automatically know what I'm talking about. "It's been a while."

"Out of practice with what?" He wasn't looking at me. His eyes were on the television above the bar, which made it a little easier to answer.

"Sex."

Then his eyes snapped to mine and my cheeks were immediately red.

He took a drink of his beer and then smiled, slightly. "Need some training, do you?"

"It wouldn't hurt, would it?"

He shrugged. He. Only. Shrugged.

So I had basically just offered up sex and he shrugged. Nice. I wanted to punch myself when I got drunk because I said shit like that and offered up anything. I'd just offered up myself on a platter to this unbelievably smoking hot guy and he fucking shrugged. If I couldn't get Destry to have sex, how in the holy hell was Silas going to even take the bait?

In a matter of ten minutes, I had five shots. For someone who doesn't drink, those five shots caught up with me quickly.

Destry shifted next to me, but surprisingly kept his cool, as always. When he didn't say anything, I continued, fearing the silence. "I... uh... sorry I said that."

"How many of those are you going to drink?" he leaned forward with his elbows on the bar, motioning toward the shot glass in my hand. Danny came by attempting to fill our shot glasses again, smiling at Destry, and then me. I'm sure it looked obvious what was happening here. Or where we were heading with this.

I held my hand up to Danny trying to cover the shot glass. "No way. I'm done."

"Ah, live a little." Danny said in a thick Canadian accent I hadn't noticed until tonight. Destry laughed beside me, nudging my elbow. I ended up uncovering my shot glass. I never wanted to lose to Destry, hence the two mile run I'd recently endured.

I looked over at Destry again, shadows danced across his cheeks when he blinked. "So how many?"

I gave him a look, a confused one at that. "Just one. Why?"

"Why not two or three more?" His eyes moved from mine to the television above the bar.

I turned on my stool and bumped his knee with mine. "Destry Stone... are you trying to take advantage of me?"

He shrugged, eyes never moving from the television but not missing a beat when he replied with, "It's just a lot easier when you make bad decisions."

Cute. No really. He's adorable.

I'm not good at flirting. Never have been. I once asked a guy while I was drunk if he wanted to go to a clam bake. That guy being Jared. That was also the night I set his car on fire and peed on his parent's living room floor. Another fabulous reason I was also still single.

"So... Destry Stone." He looked at me when I said his name, arching his brow. "What's your middle name?"

He seemed to contemplate this one for a minute and then grinned softly. "Is that really your question?"

"Well, no, I have another but I really need to know your middle name."

"It's Jacob." His face was composed when he spoke, maybe a practiced indifference he tried really hard to maintain at all times.

"Okay... Destry Jacob Stone... is boxing hard?"

He gave me a look so I squinted to be sure he was looking at me. I did just have five shots in a row. "Hard?"

"Yeah, like skill wise." Then I burst out laughing, rather loud. "Not like dick hard. Just hard.

I'm. An. Idiot.

At least he cracked a smile. It's more than what he usually offered me. "Anybody can box and throw punches. That's not hard. Landing them, and doing that round after round with the same intensity in which you started landing them, yeah, that's hard and takes years of training."

I thought about that for all of a half a second. Enough to take another drink of beer and slam the glass back down on the bar. "I think I could box." I deduced.

He laughed. Fucking laughed at me. "Yeah?"

"Oh absolutely." I screamed, because drunk me is completely tone deaf and pushed myself away from the bar just slightly and held up my fists at him. "Totally could."

Destry reached for my hand and a bottle of tequila behind the bar, smiling at me. "Let's see what you got, tough girl," he drawled out slowly, his eyelids heavy and drooping.

I returned the contagious smile that kept drawing me in tonight. "By all means, lead the way."

He led me downstairs to the boxing ring in the basement, helped me over the ropes and then stood there face-to-face with me. We both took a drink straight from the bottle and then he set it to the side.

Bouncing on the balls of his feet, he rolled his neck around. "Hit me."

I mimicked his little warm up, just trying to act like I knew what I was doing. "What?"

His teasing eyes landed on me. "Let's see what you got, tough girl."

So I did. And he let me. Crazy. I felt awful hitting him but he told me to. He provoked me.

"Fucking hell," he gasped touching his cheek and then took his gloves off. "You hit me." And for the first time since I met him, Destry's voice was playful.

"You told me to."

He smiled, dark and playful and reached for me. He shifted closer and my breath caught. The strength of his arms was never more apparent than it was right then when he picked me up like I weighed nothing.

Then I tried to wrestle him. Let me just say, ninety percent of wrestling matches between a man and woman end in sex. Always. Happened to me and Jared in college and if my memory served me correctly, that involved alcohol as well.

He pinned me to the ring, my hands raised above my head, moving his mouth to my ear and pressing his erection right where I wanted it, "I wanna show you something."

"So what are you going to show me?" I swallowed, watching his eyes, hot, dark, almost angry.

"How good sex can be..." he breathed staring at me now. His gaze on me was almost too much to take. "How good it is with me."

With me? Was it better with him? I had no doubt it probably was. Look at him.

"Who says I want to have sex with you."

His eyes narrowed. "I bet if I stuck my hand down your pants right now, you'd be willing and wet."

"And you'd be right. But I never said I wanted to have sex with you."

Liar.

Destry laughed, his chest shaking mine. "Bullshit. You've wanted to have sex with me since you saw me in the shower." He moved closer, our chest in line, blinking once but then finding my eyes again. "Have you ever been fucked?"

"Yes." I squeaked out, my eyes frantically sweeping over his chest and ending at his lips. God I want to kiss him.

His left hand moved from the floor to cradle the back of my head as he took a handful of my hair. "I'm not talking about sex, Tallan." He leaned his weight on his left elbow, then shifted sideways slightly and ran his right hand down to my hip and squeezed rocking his hips into mine. "I'm talking about sweat soaked fucking where you can't even breathe, you're just fucking. Giving them pleasure and pain to which they don't know what they like better."

"Say what?" I moaned, arching my back.

"You heard me." His lips met my skin for the first time, but never my lips, his heavy hot breath on the sensitive skin of my neck. "And by the look on your face, you're *dying* to find out."

Never stop. Never ever stop kissing my skin.

"So..." I tried to act all cool and innocent, though I was none of that and desperately tried not to rip my clothes off and scream, "Take me now!"

I didn't say that though. I kept my cool and replied with. "Are we talking about whips and chains and shit like that?"

He let out a laugh, his chest shaking me, then moved away sitting up so I was spread out before him. "Do you really think a man of my strength and endurance needs anything besides my own hands to restrain you?" He challenged raising an eyebrow.

I couldn't breathe. No really, I couldn't. He just took my ability to function with those words. I'm so in over my head.

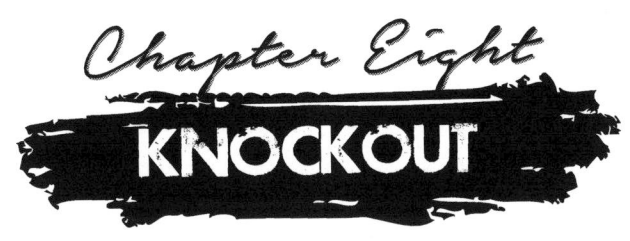

Chapter Eight
KNOCKOUT

A boxer loses by way of a knockout or KO when he or she is unable to get up unassisted after being floored by the count of ten.

A man can make you feel pretty by a look, words, or even a simple touch. They can make you feel sexy and on fire with the same. Destry had me in the throes of hot and bothered with what he'd just said to me.

Destry was making me feel beautiful in ways no man had ever done. He was worshiping me just by a stare and firm hands, and I needed that. Believe me when I say I fucking needed that. When I first came down to this basement two weeks ago I never thought I'd be having sex in this very ring. Never. Look at me already making assumptions. My plan was to get in shape so I could have sex with Silas. I'd only developed a Plan A...Plan D, also known as Destry, has thrown me for a fucking loop.

I was hopeful the moment I saw this man in the shower that I'd get to know him a little more personally. Not gonna lie.

I stared at him wondering what he was going to do next. Would he pull away? What then?

That's when he reached for the hem of his shirt and pulled it over his chest.

Fuck yeah. Now we're getting somewhere. My eyes swept over the heavenly body before me.

God, those muscles. So tight and tensed just waiting to be touched and worshiped. I could worship every long, hard muscle this man possessed. Every muscle. Oh yeah, I could.

He wasn't going to ask me if I wanted to. He knew my body wanted him. His did too, he couldn't help himself.

Had he done this before in a ring? He'd already spilled that he'd only slept with five women. Was I about to be notch number six on his heavyweight belt?

No. Don't think like that. Don't because more than likely he had. Look at him. Of course he had. He'd probably had sex in all kinds of places, up against walls, showers, in cars, on cars.

Without a word, or in my case another thought, I wrapped my legs around him. He willingly came forward but stopped, both hands on the floor next to either side of my face.

"I want you…" he breathed, watching my face react to his words. He studied me with an open intensity that caused me to gasp. He wasn't going to ask for approval, but this was my time to say no.

He watched me, and as drunk as I was, it made me uncomfortable. Like he was searching for an out, or worse, hesitating because deep down he didn't want this. My mind wouldn't stop. If you looked at Destry, and then you looked at someone like me, you'd understand why I questioned why he wanted to be here with me. I was Eve and he was the serpent telling me to eat the apple. Oh, hell yeah, give me that apple. I gave him a nudge with my legs, a silent invite to finish what he'd started. I don't think I needed to remind him that winners don't quit.

Though he still had his black Nike shorts on, he wasn't hesitating now, but he also wasn't quick about it when his hands went to my yoga pants. It was like slow motion. He stopped, his fingers curling around the edges. I looked up at the ceiling, afraid to watch as he removed my pants, open beams and florescent lights of the ceiling were my only view.

Was this really happening? Was I about to have sex with my personal trainer?

Did that scream hoochie? Of course it did.

Did that stop me? Not a snowball's chance in hell.

Destry shifted his weight, tugging my pants over my ass. When he had them off, he tossed them over his shoulder, my panties weren't far behind.

Destry, meet my pussy. She sent you a friend request a couple weeks ago.

Thanks for accepting.

My eyes traveled back to his and Destry smirked, so sexy, so sinful, as if he knew what I was thinking, and ran his hands from my hips up over my ribs and then to my breasts, cupping them. Then he went back to my hips, angled them and grinded against his. *Fuck. Just fuck!*

Tallan, meet Destry's dick. You're about to be really good friends.

His hands roamed up my sides, over my breasts and then behind my back. With just a twist of his fingers my breasts fell out of my bra on display. His eyes never left mine as his hands brushed over them and I gasped feeling my nipples harden. Destry's mouth curved into a smile, eyes trained on mine, so intent, yet, somewhat confused at the same time.

Why hasn't he kissed me yet?

I felt ridiculous being naked in front of him. Absolutely ridiculous. Like I didn't even compare to the sexiness that was him.

With his hands cupping them again, his thumbs rubbed over my nipples, and then pinched, hard as they puckered in response. My body jumped at the sensation but I didn't have time to respond when Destry replaced his mouth where his hands were. His soft tongue caressed my nipples. I was jealous of my nipples because he hadn't even kissed me yet. I moaned though, my hands flying to fist his thick dark hair, forcing his head to stay there. He certainly had no complaints and did as I asked. Rocking against my hips, I felt his erection straining to be released. He wanted this badly. But he hadn't removed his shorts.

What the fuck?

"Take these off." Raising my feet from the floor, I used them to try to pull down his shorts.

"I can't." He mumbled around my nipple, shaking his head slightly. "When I take them off, I'm fucking you. When you scream, I'm *not* stopping."

Oh, uh… damn.

Destry's mouth moved from my right nipple, to my left and then up my chest. His hands moved to cradle my head, angling it so he could kiss the exposed skin of my neck.

Damn you. Kiss me!

Teasing me some more, open mouth kisses assaulted my heated skin. I couldn't get enough and judging by his frantic movements, he couldn't either.

"Destry," I moaned. "Please, just fuck me. I'm practically begging you."

I don't know why but he truly surprised me right then.

He made a throaty sound, like a rumble from deep within and shook my body and made me shiver. "Do you know what you're asking for?" His mouth was at my jaw moving toward my mouth, slowly.

"I do, please!" More than anything, I was dying for him to finally kiss me. He'd been so close but hadn't and just when I thought he might, he pulled back. Did he have something against kissing?

When his hips pushed forward and I knew what I was missing all this time. This. Being fucked. Who am I kidding, I knew all along I was missing this.

Destry smiled, one side higher than the other, drawing back to look at me. The smile he gave me was one I hadn't seen yet, as he searched my eyes. It wasn't a playful smile, nor was it teasing or condescending. It was just a smile, almost boyish in a sense. It displayed his youth in a way I wouldn't have expected from him.

Holding my head with both hands, he leaned in, tentatively, teasing now. But then it happened.

His mouth lowered to mine, soft and gentle as his lips parted mine. Before I knew it, his tongue was pleading with mine.

He kissed me.

Destry Stone kissed me.

His kissing, much like anything else he did was full of passion. With every move he made I felt alive and the energy pulsing through me, as if he was seeping life back into me. Life I didn't even know I was missing. I whimpered, trying desperately to get closer to him as our lips went frantic, my arms wrapped around his neck. He was grabbing at my thighs, pushing himself between my legs, basically dry humping the fuck out of me as his lips did their own fucking. Our mouths went crazy, assaulting each other, tongues sliding together, lips twisting, sucking, an all in sort of kiss. My lungs ached for a breath but I wasn't willing to stop. It was the kind of kiss I would give up breathing to feel. I would die for it as drastic as that sounded.

While his hands were strong and confident as they swept over me earlier, dominating in a sense, his mouth wasn't. It's the softer side of him as long as he's not speaking. I never heard anything nice these last few weeks from his sharp tongue but his lips, they were tender, caressing, loving.

After a moment, Destry eased away, slightly, needing to breathe and I was pleasantly happy to see that he was just as breathless, panting, and incapable of saying anything. His hands did wander though, south, and exactly where I wanted them to be. Strong long fingers caressed between my legs. He pushed in, instantly wet with my arousal and he felt it. A low rumble escaped him. Pushing his fingers so deep I felt his knuckles pressing about me, I squeezed my eyes shut rolling my hips into his hand.

"You wanted this, didn't you?" Stroking me once, twice, and then he pulled away just as quickly. Slowly he brought his fingers to his mouth and then sucked on them.

Damn. Just... damn.

"Can't hide much from you, can I?"

"We're even." His voice was lower, crackling as he spoke. "I know you felt me earlier today."

Breathing slow and easy, I was trying not to give myself away too soon. He didn't need to know how bad I wanted him. Nope. He had enough going for him. I needed at least one advantage over him.

Too bad my pussy was already desperately needing to be friends with him when she saw him in the shower. Bitch gave it all away.

A sudden chill wrecked me. I wanted him. Badly. And I couldn't fight it anymore. It wrenched through my body when he kissed me again.

I smacked at his chest. "I'm being fucking serious right now. Fuck me. Right now."

I was about to rip his shorts off of him when I felt him start to pull away. I grabbed onto his concrete shoulders to make him stay, rocking my hips against his.

"I'll be right back."

I nodded, almost frantic and let go of him. Yes. Finally!

As I laid there in the ring, naked, staring at the ceiling, I started to imagine what if someone walked down here right now?

Destry was gone all but a minute and returned with a condom, but his shorts were still on.

I sat up on my elbows, eyeing him from head to toe. "Are you kidding me? Take those goddamn things off."

He smirked, again, as he ducked down under the ropes. He came closer to where I was in the middle of the ring, and started to remove his shorts but stopped leaving them hanging dangerously low on his hips so I could see the light dusting of hair and those hard ripped muscles of his stomach. And, oh, that perfect V that makes women crazy. He also had those veins popping out near his hip bones that I found so sexy on men. Damn.

My eyes then cut back to the sharp V that formed leading to where I so desperately wanted to see up close and not blinded by steam and water.

Come to me, baby.

He dropped the condom on the floor beside my hip. He wasn't moving so I got the idea that he wanted me to remove his shorts. Was he waiting for me to do it?

I took the wink he gave me as the go ahead and got on my knees in front of him. Slowly, I pulled his shorts down to his feet and then ran my hands up his long lean legs until I reached the top. Without looking at the dick in my face, saving the prize for last. I gave Destry a smile and then my eyes drifted south.

Yep. Cock model material. I knew it.

Hard, smooth, bare, perfect size, no weird kinks or bends. Just absolutely stunning.

My mouth was jealous, so I let her play. Destry knew what I was about to do and moved his hands from my shoulders to wrap around my head, once again cradling my head. When my tongue tentatively touched the head, he gasped.

I love it when men have visible reactions. It gave me the self-confidence I needed right then.

Slowly, I let my mouth glide from the tip, to base. He smelled so good, clean, like soap and laundry sheets.

When I had him all the way in my mouth, his hands gripped my hair so tightly I thought he ripped some hair out. It was clear nothing about Destry was gentle, aside from his lips. I'm not sure he knows how to be. And I'm okay with that. He warned me of that. I'm counting on it.

His hips moved on their own will, it seemed, his hands guiding my mouth over his hardness rougher than I would have expected. I gagged a few times but held my own.

He gasped. "Tell me what you want, baby."

"You," I moaned not wanting to take his dick from my mouth. I was that attached to him. "I want you, right now."

With a yank, he pulled my hair angling my head back to look at him. "How bad?"

Again, I moaned around his dick. "So bad…"

Destry couldn't wait after that, he moved me back, the sound of my mouth leaving his dick made a popping sound. He pushed back on my shoulders so I was laid flat on the ring. "I'm dying to be inside you…" he whispered. "I *need* to be. I *have* to be." His words left me blushing, skin on fire. "I can't take it any longer."

Dropping to his knees, he reached for the condom, eyes on mine, watching, waiting for me to say anything. I didn't say a word so his body came in line with mine. The weight of his strong naked body on mine took the breath straight from my lungs for a moment.

Yes. Finally!

His hands fumbled with the package before he ripped it open with his teeth. The package falls away as he took the condom in his left hand between his fingers. Rising up slightly, he looked down to put the condom on. When he finished, he looked up at me, waiting. The desire between us was mutual, a need that could only be met by this.

His slick chest slid against mine, the sensation made me shiver as his body came in line with mine again. I could feel him at my entrance, his weight leaned to the right as his left hand moved between us. He took a firm grasp on himself and moved his dick back and forth against my entrance and clit. I arched into him, the friction making me gasp, my breasts pressing into him. He took that moment to kiss across my heated skin, wet kisses that left a cool sensation in their wake.

Then, with no hesitation, he pushed forward, his hard length fully sheathed inside me for the first time.

"Oh God," I whisper, knowing there's no turning back now.

"Jesus baby, you're so fuckin' tight." Destry let out a groan, his body shaking.

I wanted to say something right then, remind him how long it'd been, but I didn't. I don't think I could actually speak.

His left hand moved and slammed against the floor beside my head, his lips traveling from my chest to my lips again. I gladly welcomed his mouth back.

When he entered me, my God was it good. A warm tingling sensation took over. His hips twitched, his body shuttering with relief of finally being inside, as if it had been a while for him too, his grip on me slipping slightly as he tried to gain control. He seemed like he wanted to, he could come at any second.

Some guys starts out slow during sex, ease into things. Others go crazy, jack rabbit the shit out of you and have your boobs bouncing so much that they are beating the shit out of your chin.

Not Destry. He fucked.

It wasn't necessarily fast, just hard, deliberate movements. Moving inside of me, skin slapping skin, eyes boring into mine, it was clear. He was fucking me. Destry Stone was fucking me. There was some aggression there. So forceful it was damn near painful but it was so good I looked past the pain.

He was right, pain could be pleasurable. I would have never known that. This was so completely different from any other sexual experience I had.

With Silas, we were young and didn't know anything.

With Jared, it was awkward. We were too good of friends and I think that ruined it for us.

Now with Destry, this wasn't either of those. He was a man. Even for only being twenty-four, he had that man quality to him. I didn't love Destry. Wasn't even sure I liked the guy. That allowed me to feel so much more in that moment. He wasn't asking if I wanted to, he knew the answer. My body had been telling him from the beginning the answer to that question.

And he wasn't waiting for me to make a move. I enjoyed that. He was very much like his fighting style. First move, all in. He didn't wait, he wasn't patient and if he saw a weakness, he reacted.

There was no hesitation on my part either. Once he kissed me it was as if my clothes peeled themselves away. I wasn't self-conscious like I thought I would be either. No. I was just horny.

It'd been way too long.

Destry didn't say much, words weren't really needed. He certainly knew what he was doing and damn if I didn't think Stella was the stupidest bitch around for letting him get away, purely on a sexual scale. I don't care how fucked up the guy was. If he could fuck like Destry, you tolerate the bullshit.

My hips grinded against his, desperate for what had been hanging in the air tonight. Release. My body was so close to the edge I could see the cliff and willingly wanted to jump.

Destry was probably the hardest person to read. I never thought I'd get a good understanding of him. Right now was completely different. The craving, the want, the desire, whatever, it's clear right then he wanted what we were doing. For someone who was so hard to judge, I could tell he wanted this as badly as I did.

After a while, the longer he moved, my body was screaming for him and he knew it. A teasing smile presented itself as he watched me. When he pulled out, he aggressively slammed back inside me, groaning as his head fell back.

I was at a loss for words at the sensations that shot through me, his forehead pressed against mine.

Every other time I've had sex has been very different from this.

Then there was Weston. A dude I met at a bar my senior year in college. He wanted me to stick my finger up his ass. I never called him back. Even went so far as to have Jared lie to him and convince him I died in a car accident.

There were others and honestly, I don't remember much about them. Just that for me, sex had never been something where I got it right the first time.

That changed when I had sex with Destry Stone. He was amazing. My pussy had for sure found her soul mate.

Part of me wondered if this was going to be quick. I wanted this to last all night. Probably because I didn't know if it would ever happen again with Destry. I hoped this wasn't simply an itch that Destry needed to scratch.

He began to move a little faster. He had endurance that's for sure.

My entire body burst into flames, it didn't need much stimulation down there but with the way this man moved, the way those powerful hips rubbed over my happy spot, damn, he could knock a bitch off quick. Within the first five minutes, my first orgasm exploded through my body, my nails digging into his shoulders.

For a moment, his thrusts that kept moving me across the ring, with my ass sliding on the floor only to have him wrap his hands up and under my shoulders, lost their rhythm and became erratic, but then he slowed, just for a second.

"Fuck, you came, didn't you? I can feel you." He muttered lowly, moving his lips to mine.

He kissed me slowly, but then the passion built and his movements and kisses became almost frantic.

"Yeah…"

I watched his muscles flex with each thrust. He fucked like he acted. With hate. But I loved it because I didn't feel like he hated me in those moments. I felt like he couldn't get enough of me. Especially with a groan that left his lips and the way one hand squeezed my neck and then the other gripped the flesh of my ass.

His head twisted, his teeth on my neck. "Fuck…" he grunted, letting out a guttural groan, teeth sinking into my skin, pleasure was most definitely painful, his body shaking, rocking against me. That's when I felt him pulsing, he was coming inside me but yet, he wasn't stopping. Clasping my hands around his neck, I could feel him still twitching when he continued his thrusts but slowed, just slightly. He came but in no way was he done. Pulling away, he ripped the condom off and then put the second on one I didn't know he'd brought with him.

His body found mine again, his wet lips moved against my neck. "One more, please…" as if he had to ask. "I can't stop."

I'd fuck this guy for days. No lie.

"Get on your hands and knees." He wasn't asking, he wasn't asking, he was demanding. "I wanna see that ass I've been staring at for weeks."

I'd been hiding that ass for weeks from his line of vision but still I did as he said, practically on command. I had absolutely no complaints. My palms slapping against the floor when he gave me a light push on my shoulders. I raised an eyebrow at him, smiling, only to have him give me a dark playful look. You know what, if he wanted to dominate me, I was all for that.

On my hands and knees in the ring, Destry placed one hand on my hips and then the other tangled in my hair. When he pressed forward, his left hand tugged on my hair pulling my body into his.

I only wished I could have seen him. I kinda felt like I was missing out since I couldn't see his face. He started out slow, grinding deep into me.

I loved this position. Each time he drove into me pushed me closer to the edge. Immediately I felt the burn and the building in the pit of my stomach. The rise came fast, that tingling in my gut and then the rush of hotness from my feet to my upper thighs as it flooded my body with endorphins. I screamed out, arching my back and then reaching behind me to grip the cheeks of my ass. Destry moved his hands from my hips to my hands and held them together in his right hand, his left pulling my hair.

After what seemed like twenty minutes, the best twenty minutes I'd ever spent with my face pressed into the canvas, he increased his pace slightly. "Is this what you wanted, Tallan? You wanted me to fuck you?"

"Yes!" My words were ripped from my throat when he pounded into me. I could barely get the words out, he was driving into me so deep and powerful that it hurt but I didn't want him to stop.

He notice and growled, "Take it. You wanted it, take it."

I worked my hips into his movements, enjoying every last sensation of that amazing orgasm when he pushed deeper seeming to enjoy that.

He let go of my hands just slightly when his hips moved faster and then he pushed down on my ass, slamming into me three more times. I turned my head slightly to see him come for a second time only his head was thrown back as he groaned. I felt him swell, every muscle tensed in his body, jaw clenched and then he jerked forward once more. Our eyes met then, his expression dark, hiding emotions I knew he didn't want me seeing. I'd give anything to know his thoughts right then.

When he pulled out, my body was shaking so badly I wouldn't be able to stand there. Good thing I was face down on the ring, my hands behind my back still in his iron grasp.

I'd been fucked for sure.

Face down, ass in the air, I was one: sore all over, and two: shaking from how I felt not having the scorching heat of his body pressed against mine.

Chapter Nine
BARNBURNER

A barnburner is a very good fight. One that is very intense and exciting, a real nail-biter. A fight that is so close it's hard to predict who will come out the winner until seconds before it ends.

Tuesday
April 19, 2011

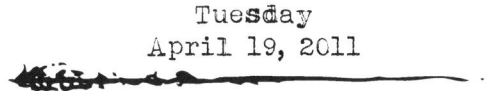

"Oh God, you had sex with him, didn't you?"

I nodded. There was no sense lying to Jared. He knew my afterglow. Sadly. There was no sense denying it. I didn't want to either. It was one of those nights I wanted to shout about from the roof tops.

He smiled and I wanted to punch him. He had this dirty grin that was actually kind of cute. And comical.

"Were you drunk?"

"Yep." I held an ice bag to my head, a bottle of water in my other hand.

An even wider smile formed. "Did you ask him if he wanted to go to a clam bake like you did to me?"

"No." I sighed getting ready to admit what I did last night. "But I tried to wrestle him and then punched him in the face."

Jared apparently thought this was the most amusing thing he'd ever heard.

"What are you going to do now?"

"I don't know. But that was the best sex of my life."

Jared, in a dramatic gesture, flopped his arms up in the air and then sighed. "You've crushed my soul!"

I reached over and patted his head, more concerned with my current situation then Jared's ego.

This was so far out of my realm. Sure I've had one night stands before but never thought about them the next day. With Destry, his touch, that roughness, his eyes, the words he said, they were never far from my mind that morning.

I honestly didn't know what I was going to do. But I had two days to think about it. My workouts were on hiatus until Thursday.

What was I doing though? Here I hired this guy, decided to write a story on him, without his knowledge, and now I was having sex with him. Or had sex with him. And now I'm really hoping that it happens again. The thought of never experiencing what we shared, again, was actually starting to depress me. But I can't be that girl. Could I? The one who slept with some random person one night and the next night was with someone else. Sure, I was horny, and yes, Destry was fan-fucking-tastic in the ring…in more ways than one…but knowing how different the sex was with Destry versus what I vaguely remember of the intimate moments five years ago that I'd shared with Silas, well, there was no comparison.

What was I doing? What was I going to do now that we'd done the deed? Was Destry expecting more from me? Was I just something he needed to get out of his system?

I'm so confused. Can I continue training with Destry with both of us *knowing* my final destination, where this would end? I can't *not* meet Silas. That part of me that he hurt so long ago wants to see if what we had even meant anything to him. But can I walk away from Destry… to meet Silas?

I'm impatient. Very impatient. When I have something to do that I'm looking forward to, I want to fast forward time. Ever since Silas called, I wanted to do just that.

Until I had sex with Destry. Now it seemed I didn't want the time to go by faster anymore. I wanted to stop it and figure out what was happening. And have sex with him again. Maybe a few times.

Thursday
April 21, 2011

I didn't work out Tuesday and Wednesday, and after that night drinking, and being with Destry, I needed that break more than ever. I never heard from him other than a text telling me to meet him at the bar at 7pm on Thursday. I wanted to reply to the text and say so much, cheesy shit like "Best night of my life!" but I also didn't want to appear too eager. I had to play this cool. I didn't want to be clingy. I needed to up my game and practice that indifference Destry was so good at.

When I met him at the bar on Thursday night, I was both nervous and excited to see him.

My heart was pounding and my hands were shaking as I walked down the stairs, the heavy black metal door squeaking as I pushed it open. My eyes remained on the concrete floor watching my steps, knowing he was down here. I was afraid to look. Flashes of our last night here swarmed around in my head. The way his hands felt over my body, the tender way he kissed me, the roughness of his touch, everything about that night was so much more than I expected it to be.

When I finally did look up, he was there, sitting against the wall with his gloves beside him, un-taping his hands, the white tape in a pile beside his thigh.

He heard the door open and looked up at me, his eyes traveling slowly up my body as my skin heated under his scorching gaze. He let out a long sigh when we looked at each other, a smile playing at his lips. "Hey."

What did that sigh mean? What did that stare mean? Did he regret it?

Just hearing his voice, immediately images of Monday night flooded my head.

"Hey." I said, returning the smile and sat next to him on the floor making sure my elbow touched his. "I, uh…" for some reason I thought I needed to explain myself for my actions Monday night. "I don't normally act like that. Must have been the vodka."

"Don't make an excuse." He sounded almost irritated that I would. Then I felt bad. "You weren't *that* drunk."

"No… I suppose I wasn't."

Destry breathed, slow and deep but kept his eyes on the ground. "Do you regret it?" He asked, quietly, with a vulnerability I wouldn't have expected from him.

"No." I don't either. Not in the slightest. "But I also don't want the awkwardness that seems to be floating around us."

He nodded, tossing the remaining piece of tape aside and then his hand rose to run up and down his jaw, as though he was thinking. When I looked over at him, waiting for him to say something, Destry laughed, lightly and then took a deep breath. "Well, let's get started then. I'm sure I can make you forget about the awkwardness."

So he didn't want awkwardness. I was cool with that because it seemed it was everywhere.

We started the workout with arms, alternating bench press, resistance band, free weights, pull ups, arm curls, and rope climbing. That part I did not enjoy in the slightest. He worked my ass off. My muscles were shaking, I was sweating so bad and my skin felt like it was two hundred degrees. Part of me didn't want him seeing me all hot and sweaty like this but his eyes were never far from my body. It gave me little hope that it didn't bother him.

Despite working my ass off, believe me when I say I watched Destry closely, wondering what he was thinking and if he regretted anything we did the other night. I doubted he did but I still couldn't help myself from being curious about it. He asked me if I regretted it, but I hadn't asked him.

Did he?

My mind wouldn't stop.

As I sat there against the wall, trying to catch my breath, Destry approached scratching his bare stomach with casualness, he smiled a beaming smile His head tipped to the door. "Let's go for a walk to stretch out your muscles a little."

"I can't run." I stood when he reached out and helped me up. "Please don't make me."

"Promise, no run. Just walking."

Watching him now, his stare on my body, I felt something more than I had in the past few years. Something stirring deep inside my gut, only it was different from all the other times. This time I was content, relaxed, and comfortable not knowing anything that could, or would happen. For a girl like me, that was rare. I had to know, but this, I was leaving it up to chance. I had no idea how Destry felt about what we did, and now, strangely enough, I was okay with that.

We ended up going for a walk, at night again. I was starting to enjoy the late night in the city. He took me up the pier instead of back to the bar, our walk slowed to a dawdling pace when our feet hit the wooden planks of the pier. A steady but easy mist started to fall but it felt good on my skin, refreshing. After all the sweating I'd done, I could taste the salt on my lips when the rain hit my skin.

He pointed toward Pier 57 brushing his damp hair from his face. "I once jumped off that pier." He chuckled, leaning over the cracked wood and peering at the darkness below. "Broke my damn arm."

I stopped beside him, our forearms touching. I inhaled, cool salty air. "How'd you break your arm?" On the water, lights flickered over the Elliott Bay creating a peaceful night, one I was used to seeing.

Destry pointed below. "There's rocks down there."

"Oh," I peeked over the side to see the shadows of large black rocks. I knew there was but most of the time the water was plenty deep enough to avoid them. "How exactly did you manage that?"

"I was ten." He shrugged hanging onto the rail and then leaning back to stretch his arms, his muscles flexing as he did so. "I didn't know you couldn't jump straight down."

That didn't surprise me. Destry seemed very much a daredevil. The kind of guy who would try anything at least once.

I'm not sure what changed in our relationship or if you could even classify anything we had as a relationship, but for the first time since I'd met him, he spoke about his dad that night. "My dad and I used to run that very same route we took." He shook his head, solemnly, but he seemed relaxed as he spoke. "Three times a week, rain or shine, it was our thing."

I knew enough from my research the last few days that James Stone, Destry's father, was still alive but in an assisted living facility since he retired from boxing eight years ago.

"Are you close with your parents?"

He seemed almost caught off guard by my question and reluctant to answer, for a moment. "My mom, she left when I was seven or eight. I don't really remember. She split about the time my dad started trying to drink himself numb. And my dad... he's not really around. He's not the same anymore. When he got sick... well, he's just not himself anymore. Not only did he never take care of his disease but he's mentally gone." Destry's eyes were distant as he spoke, focused on the water. "It feels like he's already gone."

"What happened?" I asked hesitantly wondering at what point he would shut down and tell me to mind my own business.

His shoulders slump as he leans over the wooden rail. "When I was thirteen he was diagnosed with acromegaly."

"What's that?" There wasn't any information online as to why James stepped away from boxing, just that he did. I had no idea what the reasoning was and I'd certainly never heard of this disease Destry was telling me he suffered from.

Destry stood straighter running his left hand from his hair and then replacing it on the rail. "It's a disease that results when your pituitary gland produces too much growth hormone. He has a pituitary tumor that caused it. He also has diabetes as a result."

"It causes diabetes?"

Destry shrugged. "Not always but it's common. That's not what's really given him trouble though. Acromegaly causes your body to grow, from the growth hormone. Even your internal organs grow. It's not uncommon for them to have cardiovascular problems. He had a stroke about six months ago and he can't even remember my name let alone who I am. Totally sucks."

"I'm so sorry."

He shrugged again. "Nothing you can do about it."

"So where is he now?"

"He's in a home in Bellevue where they can help him. An assisted living center. I go see him on Mondays and Wednesdays."

"Did he retire because of the disease?"

"Partly. It was argued that he had an unfair advantage because of the growth hormone being produced in his body. But in the end, he walked away on his own." Destry sighed leaning forward on the rail again, his eyes distant.

Maybe I'd overstepped there. Although I couldn't believe how open and honest he was with me all of a sudden.

He turned and nodded, "Let's get back."

We left and went back to the bar and downstairs to the basement when I reached for my bag. Part of me was anxious about leaving him now.

Honestly, I wanted to get down on my knees and beg him for a repeat.

I stood from the floor and reached for my bag, unsure of what he'd say next. "We finished?"

"No, we're not finished." Destry moved away from the wall and locked the door. "We're definitely not finished for the night."

Thank you, Jesus!

When he stepped towards me, I had to put my hands up. "I don't want to do it in the ring again. I have burns on my ass from that damn thing."

"A bed I can do," he said against the sensitive skin of my neck just below my ear.

I would do anything he wanted right then. Anything.

"Your apartment, or mine?" He asked taking a step toward me.

I practically jumped in his arms. "Mine. It's closer."

Thank God Jared wasn't there because by the time we arrived at my apartment, we were so worked up we were knocking over pictures, ran into the coffee table, dry humped against the wall and broke a cup.

Destry was all hands on and pushing me inside my bedroom door trying to rip away my clothes and his, only I was in desperate need of a shower. "I should shower."

"I could join you." He suggested hungrily, kissing up and down my neck. "Nah, no shower. I can't fucking wait any longer."

"Sure you can…" I said pushing him back against my bed. His shirt was gone, mine was ripped and his shorts were already half off, his erection evident. I still had my yoga pants on but those were being pushed off by needy hands.

"No. Fuck the shower." He sat up wrapping his hands around my waist and bringing my center to his face. "I can't. I don't care if you're sweaty. I need you… right now."

There was really no denying him when he grabbed my legs behind my knees and made me straddle him. Lying back on the bed he rocked my hips against his, sliding me along his erection. Groaning, his head tipped back, the tendons in his neck evident.

Destry was anything but gentle. And I wasn't looking for gentle when I was with him. I think he understood that. I was looking for what this heavyweight could provide.

His kiss was so damn consuming at times, like he was breathing life back into me.

Everything felt completely different this time and then my reality came crashing back. For one, I wasn't drunk. I kept trying to cover myself up, hide what he was seeing but he kept moving my hands aside and getting frustrated that I would even hide myself from him.

"Don't hide from me." He pulled back to look at me, my entire body trembled, and to be fair, his breathing was rather heavy, his eyes extremely hooded, and his chest rose and fell rapidly. "I like women, not little girls."

He had a point there, but it still wasn't easy for me. It never would be. I had this idea of what I should look like, what Destry would want someone to look like, what Silas would, and I wasn't anywhere near that image.

He smiled back at me, his eyes dropping to my lips. "You're beautiful."

My cheeks flushed and I think he was aware of the fact that I thought he was just saying that to say it. Like I was expecting him to say it.

His fingers raised my chin. "I fucking mean it."

It wasn't exactly a graceful moment of mine but I went to roll off him, and get this show on the road after hearing all that when I rolled right off my own bed.

That did nothing to distract Destry. Made him chuckle, but he helped me up and laid me flat on my mattress hovering over me.

"Condom?"

I nodded. "They're in the nightstand… but I'm on the pill. And clean. Are you?"

"I was tested a few months ago. Clean."

He was apparently okay with that and nothing more was said as he yanked his shorts down in one fluid movement and leaned back on his heel, jerking me off the bed and back to straddling his hips, my legs resting on either side on him. "Fuck me, Tallan." His left hand reached between us and slipped himself inside and then rolled us so I was on top of him. The moment I felt him inside of me again, I never wanted it to end. It was like I couldn't get enough of him. My body found something it actually craved.

"Mmm," I moaned, wrapping my arms around his neck, his lips returning to mine. I did as he said, all the while he watched me with an unfamiliar intensity.

Fuck, what is happening to me? How the hell was he managing to do this to me and make me feel this?

Destry's left hand moved from my hips and then rolled me over so he was on top of me. Soon his hands fisted my hair, and I was internally praising myself for the sounds he was making. He was obviously trying to restrain himself and it wasn't working at all.

My eyelids clenched, and I felt my stomach tingle as Destry

whispered in my ear. "You know how fucking insane you make me?" he growled, his teeth nipping at my heated wet skin as his hips forced my head into the wall. "Do you know?"

I smiled sliding my hands up his neck into his hair. "Maybe," I breathed out, hopeful that it was the truth. I wanted to make a guy like Destry go insane because it seemed like an impossible feat.

"Maybe?" he echoed, pulling back, watching my eyes. His left eyebrow rose curiously. "Haven't I made myself pretty clear here?"

I dragged my right hand from the back of his head, down his chest. "We're here, aren't we? But show me how insane I make you," I whispered. "I want to know."

Destry chuckled, shaking his head and catching my hand and putting it over my head to rest against the pillows. His hand gripped my wrist firmly while the other one stayed on my ass. The sounds he was making were coming from his chest, and I felt it resonating throughout me. He pushed harder, faster, leaning his forehead against my cheek, his hair falling in my eyes.

"Show me," I said, untangling my hands from his. "Make me feel what I do to you."

He laughed, a darker menacing laugh with undertones that seemed more threatening and less of a warning. He didn't scare me, in fact it simply turned me on even more. "Don't push me." Destry closed his eyes and groaned. His head fell forward against my shoulder, and he shook it back and forth.

I did push because it was the only way I knew right now. With him, like this, beneath him, I pushed. He took a firm grasp on my hip with the hand that wasn't tangled in my hair bringing his soft wet lips down on my shoulder, biting and kissing his way along the top of my collarbone.

I pushed and he pinned, easily keeping my hands from him and overpowering me like only he could do. "Do you know what I'm capable of? The pain I can cause?" His breathing felt as shallow as my own. He was so far past being in control, every bit as defenseless and dependent as me.

There was something in his words I didn't understand though. A deeper meaning. I had a feeling the pain he spoke of wasn't physical.

Despite me pushing him, he moved at his own pace, holding me tight, dropping his voice as his body rocked against me. He knew exactly what he was doing. His words, his touch, his kisses were everywhere, showing me exactly what I had been missing and what I was now looking forward to every time I saw him.

It was somewhere after my third orgasm when I could tell he was moments away from his release by the tensed expression and lust-hooded eyes that held me in his grasp.

His hands came up to wrap around the back of my shoulders and pushed me down on him once more. With another forceful thrust, I could feel him releasing inside me as he bit down on my shoulder, crying out at the sheer force and magnitude of his orgasm. I tried to get a look at his face, but his head was buried in my neck, succumbed to the sensations rocking through him.

I wanted, no I needed, to see that glorious moment of release. I loved watching his contorted expression in the glimpse I got of it last night.

He groaned again as he buried his face in my neck and made me scream as his body shook above mine. Moaning, curving into me as his knees spread my legs farther, his hips jerked forward. I could feel him harden, still grunting in my ear as he trembled, his warmth filling me. "Fuck ..."

I sighed, my mind completely swarming. I was afraid to move or even breathe. Staring at my ceiling, I waited for him to move, or say something. Raising my hand, I pushed my hair from my slick face.

Drawing in a shaky breath, he whispered, "A shower might be good now." Still panting, he placed a row of soft tender kisses along my collarbone.

We both showered and that led to more sex, which I was okay with.

I wasn't sure if he would leave after that, but he surprised me when he laid on my bed, the moon light coming in through the cracks in the curtains since we'd been up most of the night fucking. When I glanced at him, I could vaguely make out his expression in the dim lighting.

Lying on his back, wearing his basketball shorts but no shirt, arms contently resting on his stomach, I studied his breathing searching for the unevenness I felt. His left hand rose to run through his hair, blinking he continued to stare at the ceiling. Damn it. I really wish I knew what he was thinking.

What really caught my attention was the intensity marking his stare as he focused on nothing in particular. There seemed to be a restlessness, a vulnerability that I might never understand. Seeing that, I couldn't stop my mind from convincing me he'd regret what we've done.

Eventually his eyes drifted closed and I wondered if he was just going to sleep here. I wouldn't care, but I couldn't sleep. My mind was racing as it usually did. Most of the time it took me hours after lying in bed to finally sleep. As quietly as I could, I pulled out my notebook and wrote down a few notes.

There's something to be said about a man who can throw punches with tenacity, land them with intensity, and do that round after round. As I sit in the dimly lit room that dwarfs the ring where this heavyweight title holder had trained for years, I'm reminded that he's much more than just a fighter.

Eventually, my body succumbed to the long day and I got tired. Around four that morning I laid down on the bed next to him. Destry stirred, his eyes opening and searching mine.

When he looked over at me, those moments, this one right now whether you were in them or not, where you felt something more than what you *intended* to feel, more than what you *wanted* to feel, that was right now.

He was going to say something as he pushed my hair from my face but it seemed to take him a moment to find his voice.

"See you later tonight," his voice was anxious as he whispered in my ear, then kissed my forehead. Moments later I heard my bedroom door open, the sting of his heated lips still lingering on my skin. He just left and with it took one more shred of doubt with him as I worried about what I was doing in this situation.

Chapter Ten
COUNT

A count is tolling of the seconds by the referee after a boxer is knocked down. If a boxer is still down at the end of the count of ten then the fight is over by knockout.

Friday
April 22, 2011

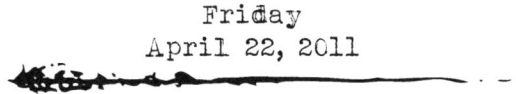

I laid in bed that morning afraid to move. I hurt, everywhere. Worse than workout pain and the soreness between my legs was unreal.

I had to get up though since I needed to meet Marcus for lunch. And maybe tell him I couldn't do this article. Not after what Destry and I had shared, I couldn't betray his trust and write something that may or may not cause him more drama in his life. Whatever happened the night of that fight, Destry wasn't talking so I knew it had to be a big deal and whatever I'd uncover about that night could make or break an already somewhat broken man. Marcus was going to have to understand that it wasn't about a story here, it was about a man, a man I was afraid I was falling for.

"You're up early." I said greeting Jared who was sitting at the table with coffee and the paper. Destry had left maybe an hour ago and I couldn't sleep so I decided coffee was needed.

"Yeah, someone had to help Destry when he locked himself out of our apartment and left his keys on the table."

"Oh, he never knocked, did he?"

"No, but I was on the couch when he came out of your room and then he forgot his keys. I heard him trying to open the door and I answered the door with my gun." Jared smiled. "Scared the shit out of him."

"Oh my God," my hand covered my mouth. "You didn't?"

"Yeah, I did."

"What did he say?"

"Same thing everyone says. Don't shoot." Jared saw the concert tickets on the counter. "Tallan, seriously, are you still thinking of meeting Silas?"

"I don't know."

"And you're paying Destry. And fucking him. That's like prostitution." He pointed out. "I could arrest you for that."

"Shut up." I groaned pouring myself another cup of coffee and sitting at the table with him.

Jared laughed, shifting the conversation. "I'm being serious. I think you should tell him about the article."

"No shit."

"Seriously."

"I'm going to when the time is right." I had no problems talking to Jared about my personal life. I also, in a strange sense, needed his approval in a way that what I was doing wasn't completely wrong. Or I guess I wanted his take on Destry as a person. He was very good at judging character. He had to be with his job. "What do you think of him?"

"He's cool." He didn't hesitate to say. "Wasn't very talkative when he left at four this morning but he seemed like he wasn't a complete tool."

As we sat there drinking coffee, me with my black sugarless coffee and him with a mocha I would quite possibly kill him for, he asked, "Have you asked him what's going on with you two?"

"No. I don't want to. I'm afraid of what he'll say." I admitted. "What if he says it's just sex? What would I say then?"

Jared leaned forward, his elbows resting on the table, his hands wrapped around his coffee mug. "Do you want more than sex?"

"Maybe." I shrugged. "I don't know."

"Well, I saw him this morning. It's more than sex."

I wouldn't allow myself the notion that what we had meant anything more to Destry. It scared me that it might. It scared me more that it might not.

"How do you know?"

"I'm a guy." Jared pointed out, as if this should have been completely obvious to me. "I know these things." I gave him a look so he continued. "He was reluctant to leave. That's how I know. He opened your door and stood there, like he was contemplating staying. If it was just sex, there'd be no hesitation."

I contemplated that but I didn't want to get my hopes up. "Have you seen Catie lately?"

"Don't do that." Jared stood reaching for his coffee cup and then took it with him as he walked towards the sink.

"Do what?"

"Act like what I'm doing with Catie is similar to this." He set his cup in the sink and then turned to face me.

I shifted my position in the chair so I was facing him. "Well… isn't it?"

"No." He shook his head crossing his folded arms over his chest. "Not at all."

"How so?"

Jared smiled. "I'm not paying her."

Jared went to work that morning and I went in my room and got dressed with a pair of gray leggings I bought the other day, a light blue sweater and black boots. It'd been a while since I dressed like this but something had me feeling comfortable. How was it possible that the fat girl from a few weeks ago was now comfortable in gray leggings and could fit the 'cankles' Jared had so rudely pointed out into black boots?

I owned this look. The past few weeks I'd found myself again. Destry not only had helped me physically, but he'd relieved me of a lot of emotional baggage I'd been carrying around about the way I looked simply by being attracted to me at what I considered my worst. There wasn't a chance in hell that I'd be able to write an article about this man without betraying his trust. Marcus was just going to have to understand.

I met Marcus at the same restaurant as before and noticed it was right around the corner from Destry's apartment. Maybe I should sneak over there for a quickie?

What the hell is wrong with you?

Stop it. Focus.

On the bus ride over there I found myself checking Twitter to see if Silas had updated anything. The only Tweet was one with him and his band in Texas at a show last night. He looked good. Smiling and relaxed, and I found myself smiling too.

When I entered the restaurant, Marcus smiled and stood when I approached the table. He was also such a gentleman. But I'll be honest here, I wanted to punch him because of the pressure he was putting on me to write this article.

We took a seat. "You look great, Tallan."

"Thanks." I paused and took a drink of the ice water already on the table. "I can't do the article." There was no sense in beating around the bush. I had to be honest. With someone.

"What?" He panicked, his eyes wide. "Why?"

Resting my elbows on the table, my hand covered my mouth slightly. "I'm in too deep."

Marcus stared at me. I've known Marcus for a while now. Now he doesn't know me as well as Jared does, but he knows me pretty well. Nothing short of subtlety, he then said, "You slept with him."

I sighed resting my forehead on my clasped hands. "I don't know why I try to hide anything."

Casually Marcus looked over the menu, his eyes lifting to mine momentarily. "So why does that change anything?"

"Because. He willingly started offering up information to me. Personal information. Now I feel like I'm using him."

Marcus shrugged setting down his menu. "You kind of are."

I kicked him under the table. Immediately he hunched forward and grabbed his leg. "I am not! And if I am, it's because of you, asshole." I slammed my fist on the table shaking water glasses. "I'm. In. Too. Deep."

I calmed down slightly after ordering our meals and I started snacking on my veggie and hummus plate that tasted like a dog's ass.

"I feel like I'm breaking his trust. I need to tell him about the article."

Marcus considered this for a moment, but then said, "If you do, be prepared for him to shut down and not tell you anything. And you are also running the risk that he won't have anything at all to do with you ever again."

Was losing what I had with Destry now worth it?

But then again, what is it that I have with him aside from hot sex and a personal trainer?

I wasn't sure I wanted to actually put a name or a category to what we have. For now, it was what worked for me, maybe even for him. But the concert and my six week deadline was fast approaching. I've got bigger problems to face in my future than telling Destry about this article. When Destry's personal training work was completed, was I going to be able to walk away from everything that we'd shared to walk into the arms of another man?

Before I left, Marcus caught me by the arm. "Does this mean you're giving up on it? You won't do the article?"

I sighed, contemplating it. Giving up? Of course I couldn't give up. Marcus knew what to say to me. I hate myself for it at times but challenge me and I become dedicated to the cause.

"I'll do the article… but it's not going up on your blog until he approves it."

Marcus gave me a weak smile, his hand rubbing over his jaw. "Good luck with that."

Thursday
April 28, 2011

Destry ended up having to move our workouts around, and cancel a couple because his dad wasn't doing well. They apparently had to do some kind of procedure on him but Destry didn't say what and wasn't willing to talk about it. He was at Virginia Mason in the ICU for now.

On Thursday, after our work-out, I figured judging by his mood he'd want some time alone. Never did I think he'd invite me back to his apartment.

Maybe he needed a distraction. I was apparently his distraction.

We were sitting on his couch, the *Rocky* movie playing on his large flat screen while we ate take out from Jade Garden. The wild mushroom roasted chicken they served was something I could eat every night. No lie.

We made small talk as we ate, when he surprised me by asking about Jared. "How long have you lived with that guy?"

I chewed slowly and then reached for my napkin covering my mouth as I spoke. "Since we graduated from college."

Destry took a bite of his chicken, then asked, "He's a cop?"

"Yeah." I laughed trying to cut my chicken with those stupid plastic knives that don't cut meat worth a damn. "Did he scare you the other night?"

Destry chuckled. "At first. He was holding a gun."

"What about you." I gave up on the knife and pushed my food away setting it on the coffee table in front of us. "You live alone, right?"

I knew after being here last time he only had a one bedroom apartment but you never know. I mostly just wanted to hear him say he wasn't seeing anyone.

"Yes. I used to live with someone but she moved out. My dad lived with me for a few months but it was clear I wasn't what he needed. I let him stay in my room and I slept on the couch for a few months. After I found him wandering the halls looking for my mom, I decided it was time he went somewhere they could keep better track of him."

"So then you put him into that assisted living center?"

He nodded setting his empty container on the coffee table next to my food. "It's just better that way. Now he gets the care he needs."

Destry's mood shifted, his elbows resting on his knees as he stared at the television. My attention wasn't on the movie. It was on this man next to me and how he got to be this reserved and closed off. There's so much more to him. I already knew I was probably the first person he'd talked about any of this with in possibly two years.

"One woman fucked you up, didn't she?"

Oh God, why did I just ask that?

Destry sat back against the couch running his hands through his hair considering my question. "You could say that."

Bringing my legs up, I rested my chin on my knees hugging my legs to my body. "That Stella girl?"

Just the mention of her name caused him to flinch. The words seemed to hang there in the air and for a brief moment I wanted to take them back. Maybe I shouldn't have mentioned her.

"I was with her for two years. Never once did I fuck around on her." He shrugged and I could tell his confession about her was difficult. "Then she fucked me over."

My eyes dropped from him to my hands. "I know exactly how that goes."

"Yeah, I bet you do." He said honestly, seeming a bit short with his words. Ordinarily I'd say he was being rude, or condescending but not right now. He was being honest. He really did understand how I felt. "I… I can't blame her for leaving. I was a dick and I wasn't the easiest person to get along with. That part I don't blame her for. What I do blame her for was *how* she did it, and *when*."

I lifted my eyes back to his. "At your fight?"

"Yeah, she walked out the moment I was knocked out. In front of everyone." He shifted his position on the couch and leaned toward me. "The thing is, I fight for what I love. I would have fought for her. But she never gave me the chance. She gave up on us long before that fight."

There was an intense part of the movie, a fight scene with Rocky and another guy that caught Destry's eyes. "Why did you give up boxing?"

"I didn't give up." He shook his head looking away from the television but not at me directly. "I'm just waiting for my time to prove them wrong."

I'm not sure what that meant, or that I even understood it. For the most part, I believed, as I've seen, Destry didn't say anything he didn't mean.

"I've heard people say you threw the fight... lost on purpose... did you?"

He hesitated before answering. "People have their theories. Everyone thinks I gave up all because I lost the title. That's not true. I didn't. I just... I walked away to give myself time to find me." He swallowed and cleared his throat. "Somewhere along the way I forgot why I loved boxing and was doing it for a purse."

He never directly answered the question but I didn't expect him to.

"And have you? Have you found that reason?"

I was beginning to understand that Destry didn't talk just to talk. When he spoke, his words were chosen carefully and said with patience. Sometimes he'd take these long pauses before speaking just to find exactly what he wanted to say. He smiled, softly. "I'd say I'm closer than I was four weeks ago."

I smiled too, hoping that meant me, but not wanting to get my hopes up.

My eyes drifted around his bare apartment again and I wondered why he didn't have any photographs around. I wasn't exactly close with my family, only because they drove me nuts half the time. I knew from my research he was an only child, like myself, but wasn't sure if he had anyone close to him. "Do you have any family besides your dad?"

"I have Danny." His reply was snorted, as if Danny was family but not one he liked to recognize.

Through an awkward conversation one night with Danny, his uncle, while I waited for Destry, he told me about Wes Callahan, Destry's childhood best friend but he left out a lot of details. Danny was really good at telling everyone's business, but his own.

"And Wes Callahan, was he your trainer?"

"No. Adam's my trainer. That guy who's always there in the ring with me. Wes… he…" His eyes drifted to mine. I could tell by his gritty voice that he was either annoyed, or curious as to how I knew about Wes. He started to say something and then cleared his throat. "He used to be my manager. And my best friend. I'd known him since I was a smartass kid."

"You're still a smartass," I laughed, "but what happened between you guys?"

Destry's brow scrunched as he scratched the side of his face with the back of his hand. "How do you even know about Wes?"

My heart started pounding. Shit. Maybe Danny wasn't supposed to tell me. "Danny told me that he used to be your manager."

He nodded. "Well, last year, after my fight with Ray Lucas, he took about two-hundred grand from me and I haven't seen him since."

"Jesus, Danny didn't say anything like that."

"Wes is gonna need Jesus when I find him and Danny needs to keep his fucking mouth shut and mind his own goddamn business."

"What's with him anyways?"

"Danny?"

"Yeah."

"Danny's a fucking loser." Destry sighed. "Fucking guy can't stop betting his life and marriages away. I own that goddamn bar—and his house—and he's constantly getting in deep. It'd be a blessing if one of those sharks broke his hands so he couldn't place the bets." He raised an eyebrow at me. "Don't think I haven't been tempted to do it myself."

"So you're kind of like, taking care of him?"

"Yeah," he sighed, "When my pops got sick, he asked that I look after him. It's his kid brother and he'd be crushed if anything happened to him. But the guy just doesn't know when to say enough is enough. He's always trying to get the easy money. Life doesn't work that way."

I wanted to lighten the conversation. I had to. He seemed almost sad. I could deal with an angry Destry. I could deal with him teasing me too. What I couldn't deal with was his sadness. No way. It was too much for me. I once saw Jared cry when his dad died two years ago and it about did me in. I think I was more of an emotional wreck than he was.

So, given this state of mind, I blurted out, "Did you really know I was in the locker room that night? I've been dying to know that."

Destry gave me a sigh, I'm sure thankful for the subject change, and nodded. "Yep. When I leaned back against the wall, I saw you."

I was so embarrassed. My cheeks flushed a bright red as I covered my face with my palms. "I can't believe you let me watch."

He gave me a careless shrug nudging my leg with his knee. "Why not? You enjoyed the view, right? I sure as hell enjoyed having you in my line of sight."

I gave him a nod. Nothing else. Just a nod. I was too scared to say anymore.

He chuckled and then swooped me up in his arms making me sit on his lap. "Tell me, did you?"

"It was…" I paused running my hands over his jaw. "The hottest thing I've ever seen in my life."

Next thing I knew, he kissed me with the same intensity he always did. Pulling back, he cradled my face in his hands pushing my hair from my face. I was expecting him to say something, but he didn't. He only stared at me, like he was overcoming some sort of emotion.

He stood from his place on the couch and reached for my hand. I went, standing next to him with my chest pressed against his. "Wanna take a shower with me?" His face was close to mine, breath on my neck, grunting with each push. His strong hands on my body were so rough with need that it took me a moment to respond, to comprehend someone wanting me as much as Destry did in those moments.

"Yes." I smiled. I knew where this was going.

Fuck yeah, I wanted to take a shower with him again. Especially if it was anything like our last one.

We made it inside his bathroom but then stood there, waiting for the water to warm up.

There's these moments with Destry when he looked at me and I felt something more. I felt like there was something behind those eyes that tried so hard to practice and maintain an indifference. At times, it wavered. He would blink and it was gone, like a flash. Was it even there?

Reaching out, his hands cupped my face. My body reacted and leaned into his chest. My hands went to his hips reaching for the hem of his shirt. Keeping my eyes locked with his, I pulled his shirt over his head, my hands moving at a dawdling pace. I let it fall to our feet. He wasn't as gentle fisting my tank top at my sides. It was gone just as quickly.

While he moved his hands back to my face, bringing my kiss to his, mine went to his shorts slipping my hand inside. Already hard, he thrust his hips into my palm. The steam rolled around us but neither made an attempt to get in the shower. Sliding my hands over his length, he got frustrated, grabbing my wrist and jerking it away.

"Get in the shower." He growled giving me a push, a light one.

The rest of our clothes were removed quickly and I was lifted into the shower.

I knew where this would lead but when he was under the spray, I reached for the soap, squirted a generous amount in the palm of my hand and then wrapped my hands around his waist and to his dick that was still hard.

I stroked him once, twice, soapy hands gliding over his hard length but I hadn't done any more. He wasn't happy.

"Tallan." He shook his head, menacing eyes narrowed and raked down my body. "I warned you... I don't like being teased."

A sudden bolt of pleasure shot through me tingling the pit of my stomach. If it meant he showed me a side he never showed anyone, I would tease him over and over again.

He didn't hesitate, his iron grip moving me. That's when he moved to stand behind me, nudging my legs apart with his legs. Distracting me with wet seductive kisses over my shoulders, he bent forward, grasping both my wrists, and placing them on the wall of the shower.

I turned to look over my shoulder at him when he entered me, moving slowly at first, his jaw clenched.

My cheek was pressed into the tile, my breasts slapping against it. Water sprayed my face as Destry frantically pounded into me. I felt like I was making so much noise that everyone in his apartment complex could have heard me. Destry wasn't any quieter. His hands glided across my ass, then his thumb pressed at my rear entrance. "Let me?"

Oh. Uh.

"Do you have any… lube?"

Destry didn't meet my eyes but he pulled out and moved the shower curtain aside to lean over the sink beside the shower. I watched his muscles as he fought to keep himself steady while digging through the drawers under the sink.

He found what he was looking for and then smiled. "This should work."

It was Vaseline. Hmmm.

I gave a nod, trying to erase the memory of the last time I did this. Surely Destry would know what he was doing back there.

Dipping two fingers into the container, he placed a quarter sized amount of Vaseline on him. I'd straightened out by then, standing beside him, my hands on my hips when he smacked my ass. "Turn around."

I did as he said placing my hands back on the tile wall. That seemed to please him, his body hunched over mine as he slid his hardness up and down against the crack of my ass, once, twice, I moaned. "That's it, baby," he growled, "do as I say."

He's so dirty and I love it. Fucking love it.

He pulled back after kissing the side of my neck. Teasing me, he slid his dick back and forth. I shuttered out a breath when he got the tip in. "Oh God…"

"Fuck baby… so fucking tight." His arms tightened around my hips, another tangled in my hair forcing my head back slightly.

I couldn't breathe. He wasn't as rough when he entered me, slowly sliding inside a hole I used to be adamant was an exit only.

I found my breath again, only I slipped when my footing shifted and my hips pushed back until the cheeks of my ass met his hips. His body slumped forward at the shift, all the way sheathed inside of me and pushing deeper. I felt myself stretching around his hard length. It burned.

It was painful, but my body was screaming with sensations I'd never felt before. Forcing myself to relax, that's when it started to feel good. That burning started to fade and though it was great, it wasn't horrible.

Destry slid his left hand over my thigh and between my legs, trying to ease my discomfort. "Just relax." I think he could tell I was in pain as my body trembled. "If you relax, it will feel good. I promise you."

"Is this the pleasurable pain you spoke of?" I turned my head over my shoulder to look back at him.

He considered that for a moment, the gaze he let loose on me was intense, much like any other gaze I got from him. "Part of it."

Part of it? Was there more?

I felt his grip on my hip tighten, his body trembled slightly but his hand moved between my legs, easily sliding along my clit, twisting, circling. The man knew how to work his hands. It was the force of his hips, the way he stretched me, made me feel things I've never ever felt before. "Fuck me, Destry. Fuck me hard!"

Who am I? What the hell has happened to me?

He slammed into me, restraint obliterated, harder than before, my head hitting the tile wall. He lifted his right leg up and propped it against the edge of the tub for leverage and goddamn did he fuck me. I forgot all about that pain. All I felt was the raw need this man was ripping out of me.

"Come for me." He whispered, slamming into me again.

His grunts, my moans and the sounds of wet skin slapping against each other filled the room. Steam floated around us as my orgasm shook through me. The desperation in his grip on my hip increased as he pounded in to me, chasing his own orgasm. "I'm… gonna come. Do you want me to pull out?" his voice was strained, barely audible.

I shook my head. "No," I moaned, "come inside me."

The next second, his body jerked forward and bent over me as his orgasm rocked through him.

Continuing to move slowly, I could feel him panting against my back, his hot breath creating a rush of pleasure through my body again making me shake.

My body tingled all over. From my toes to the backs of my legs, a soreness set in as he pulled out. I felt fucked, in a lot of ways.

I was off balance when he slid out, seeing stars and a little faint. I grabbed onto his shoulders for balance. He sighed, his face buried in my neck. "I got you."

Entangling myself from him, I stood against the wall as he reached for the soap. Turning to face me, he ran the tips of his fingers over my collarbone and then smiled, one side higher than the other.

Yep. Stella was a fucking idiot for ever leaving this guy.

"That was…" I didn't have words.

"Amazing?" He finished, a certain amount of pride in his voice.

"I don't think I'll be able to walk tomorrow." I mumbled staring down at the water beading on my skin, red marks on my hips from where his grip was.

Destry laughed as he reached for the shampoo and started washing his hair. "That could be arranged," he winked, "if you're looking for that sort of thing."

It was then, looking at him with that playful look, I didn't want to lie to him. He needed to know but I couldn't say the words.

"Did it hurt?" His eyes were kept low, and then lifted to meet mine.

"Yes. It did but it wasn't horrible."

"Have you done that before?" He looked me up and down, his voice a soft murmur. I was starting to hate it when he did that. Made me feel like he was searching for answers to questions he wasn't asking.

"Yes, but it never felt like that."

He gave a nod, but nothing more.

I couldn't stay, not that I was assuming he would ever want me to, but I had to get out of there after that shower sex. This was our third time together and it wasn't getting any easier. I really enjoyed sex with him. It was amazing, like nothing I'd ever experienced before.

But was it just sex? When did it end?

I hired him for six weeks. And now I was fucking him. Doing it once, I could understand that I was sexually frustrated. Twice? That's pushing it. Three times? That's a little much.

I hesitated leaving as I stood by his door, my bag in hand. I think he knew I was having some internal bantering so he helped me out.

His lips brushed mine, just softly. "See you tomorrow." And then he leaned into the door frame, sexy as hell.

I spun around and left. I had to.

When I got back to my apartment, Jared was up, door unlocked, lying on the couch with a beer in one hand and a remote in the other. It was nearing one that morning, why he was still up was beyond me.

I was on the verge of tears when I opened the door. Despite dieting, I reached in the freezer, grabbed the container of chocolate ice cream and two spoons.

When I stepped toward the couch, Jared sat up and gave me room. I sat next to him, put my head on his shoulder and handed him a spoon.

He took it. "Rough night?"

I shifted, my ass was sore. Ordinarily I might have told Jared that Destry and I had sex again. Only he knew.

"You're in over your head with him, aren't you?"

"Probably." I stuck my spoon in the ice cream. "What am I going to do, Jared?"

"Stop having sex with him." He took the container of ice cream from me and set his beer on the coffee table in front of us.

"I'm not sure that it's something I can walk away from that easily."

We both took turns taking bite after bite of the ice cream when he asked, "Did you tell him about the article?"

"No. I just think he… well, if I can get him to read it after I finish it, he'll think differently."

"You hope he does. What if he doesn't?"

"I don't know." Honestly, deep down, I'd already convinced myself that I could handle this.

"And you're still going to the concert?"

"What's with all the questions? I just want to sit here and eat ice cream with my best friend. Stop hounding me like a chick."

Jared rolled his eyes and ripped the ice cream container from my hands. "I don't want to see you get hurt. That's all."

I understood what Jared was trying to do. I did. But I had no idea how to deal with any of this. Here I hired the guy to train me, so hell-bent on losing weight and now none of that seemed to matter after one night with him. Okay three.

He went from being a dick, to giving dick. My biggest dilemma seemed to be that Destry had opened up to me. He was trusting me. That's when I was starting to have doubts about being able to handle it.

Chapter Eleven
INSIDE FIGHTER

An inside fighter or infighter gets in close, tries to close the gap between himself and his opponent then he overwhelms his opponent with a flurry of hooks and uppercuts. Inside fighters have to be quick and masters of counterpunching.

Monday
May 2, 2011

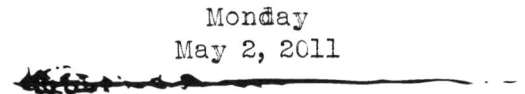

Usually when I woke up, I was sore these days. That still hadn't changed but a few weeks with Destry and it was a new kind of sore. It'd been replaced with a good sore. One I'd gladly take.

His dad was back at Stratford. It was clear Destry had spared no expense to make sure his dad was comfortable. Part of me, all right, all of me was nervous going there. I had no idea what to expect when I entered the building but there was a tall slender woman seated at the front desk, her glasses pushed down lower on her narrow nose. She reminded me of Julia Roberts with her wide smile and long red hair that was pulled over her right shoulder.

"Can I help you?" She didn't look up until I was at the counter, then her bright smile was delivered toward me.

"I'm here to see James Stone."

"And you are?"

Shit. I never thought about it before but I bet I wouldn't be able to see him. "Tallan Spencer."

Her smile never faded. "Are you a friend of the family?"

"Yes. I'm friends with his son, Destry."

"Oh," she sighed, her eyes taking on a sudden warmth. "We just love Destry. He's so sweet."

She must have him confused with someone else. Unless he's slept with her too.

Jesus, Tallan, don't think like that!

"Well," the woman stood after having me sign in, "James is having a good day. He'll be excited to have a visitor.

She then led me down a hallway towards the elevators where we went to the fourth floor. His room was the third door on the left with a slate gray name plate that read "Stone" in black letters.

The woman turned to me sweeping her long hair over her right shoulder again. "I'm Maggie by the way. Let me know if you need anything." Then she knocked on the door lightly before opening it. "Mr. Stone, Tallan's here to see you."

Oh great, she announced me like we were long lost buddies.

What the hell was I going to say to him?

"Hey, I'm Tallan. I've been having sex with your son. Nice to meet you. Now tell me, why is he so complicated?"

None of that was going to be said. For good reason.

When the door opened, I was surprised to see James sitting by the window in a wheel chair. I did some research the other night on acromegaly when Destry told me James had that. My research didn't provide all that much in the way of appearances, other than extreme cases.

James didn't look anything like that. Though he appeared tall, around six foot five, maybe taller, he did have the extended jaw and widened forehead they spoke of. But definitely wasn't the extreme cases that were detailed online.

Maggie left and James looked over his shoulder at me scratching the side of his head. For being fifty-eight, he appeared a lot older. Destry definitely took after his father in his looks in many ways. Though his hair was now gray and thinning, he had those remarkable green eyes and the same indifferent stare. So maybe it didn't always have to do with Destry. Or, maybe James was trying to protect himself too. He was dressed casually in a gray long sleeve shirt and black slacks that met a pair of black dress shoes, his feet propped up on the wheelchair. He looked healthy from what I could see, not someone who had just spent a week in the hospital.

"Can I help you, honey?" He asked, watching me enter his apartment. The door closed behind me. That's when I realized I really shouldn't have come here.

My hands shook as I took a seat across from him on a black leather couch. "I'm Tallan Spencer, sir. I'm a friend of Destry's." I reached out to shake his hand.

He hesitated, maybe trying to recall me, and then held out his hand that looked to be twice the size of mine, no doubt a product of the disease.

"Nice to meet you." He said, smiling at me. Yep, definitely Destry's father.

"Same here."

And then came, "Do I know you?"

Shit.

"Well, no…" I tried to appear casual but he had to have wondered who I was and why I was in here. "I just came to see if you needed a friend. Sometimes it's nice to have visitors."

"Oh." He nodded and looked out the window he was sitting in front of. "That's nice of you."

"Do you have visitors often?" I was trying to make small talk. Anything to keep him from wondering who I really was and calling security on me.

"I have a boy who visits me often."

"Your son?"

"No." he shook his head. "I have a son. He was the greatest part of my life."

"But you don't seem him anymore?"

"No." Again, he shook his head, his hands fidgeting in his lap. There was a distant look in his eyes that seemed to be marred with confusion. He was trying to remember and couldn't.

"What's his name?"

"Destry. He's the world heavyweight champion." His eyes drifted to me. "My boy, he's a rare fighter in today's world. Not only does he not trash talk, he's a southpaw."

"And that's rare?"

"Yes. Very rare. Some say fighters are at a disadvantage being a southpaw and need to learn to fight right handed. Not Destry. Never." His voice was raised and it was clear just talking about his son gave him great pleasure.

"That's amazing."

James smiled, content just sitting here talking about his son. "He worked so hard for that title. His first fight was November 11, 2004. He'd just turned eighteen. Two years later on his twentieth birthday, August 11, 2006, he won the WBO title against Stefan Aksakov in Japan."

James picked up a photograph, one of many around his apartment, and handed it to me. "That's my boy when he was seven."

He was absolutely adorable. You could see right then he hadn't always been an asshole. Life had made him that way. "That's his mother next to him. She left six months after that. I was a drunk and an asshole. She had every right to leave us. And Destry suffered because of that. She walked out on him too."

Now more than ever I understood his apprehensions. Not only did his mother leave, Stella did too.

Don't you dare hurt him, Tallan.

I must have talked to James for close to two hours before Maggie came back. "James, would you like to come down for lunch?"

"Oh," James took the photograph back when I handed it to me. "I guess I should eat."

Maggie came in, smiled at me and then retrieved medicine from the fridge before approaching James. She began to wheel him away when he grabbed my hand. "It was nice talking with you, honey. Please come back sometime."

I reached down and patted his shoulder, winking at him. "I

definitely will."

My heart broke for James. The way he couldn't remember anything about right now. In many ways, he's stuck, never moving on from the memories he had. That had to be depressing because everything you ever did wrong would always haunt you. There's no moving on.

I shouldn't have went there but something made me go see James. I felt like to understand Destry, I had to see his father and see what Destry saw every day. It only complicated it for me. It made me feel something more for him.

Whenever Destry said his dad's name, there was a tiny glimmer of pain he tried so hard to keep hidden, but I saw it. It was in the way his hands shook when he talked about him in the ICU and the distant look that took over his eyes when he said his name.

As I was leaving, I looked back at him and he smiled. Just smiled.

I'll never understand this, but why was it that people who were dying constantly thought about living? They wondered what they could have and what they would have done differently.

I believed people could be living, but really dying—depression, disease, or just miserable for no reason.

Then there were people dying but living. They were living their last days to the fullest, because they know they have to, experiencing and believing they had given it everything they had to give, knowing inside their heart they'd never truly die.

That was who I wanted to be. I wanted to have the dying but living attitude.

When I met Destry, I was living but dying. And that had gone on for years for me, because I had let it. Too many years if you asked me.

After meeting James, I walked away with one thought...I understood that you don't have control over your life. But you do have control over how you live it.

It was nearing workout time when I got back so I grabbed some food on the way to the bar. Luckily we were working on arms so I didn't feel like I would throw up if I ate before working out my legs.

Adam had just left when I saw Destry still standing in the ring, no shirt on, black shorts and black gloves. With his hands draped over the top rope, his eyes lifted to find mine.

He didn't say anything, not that I expected him to. I've been curious about his training. What gets me is the ferocity and accuracy he puts into just throwing a punch. There's no down time when a boxer is training either. He's literally in the gym every day. He has to be.

I stepped toward him and set my bag down. He watched me as I stepped inside the ring with him. Standing, he turned to face me letting his gaze linger in all the places his mouth assaulted my skin last time.

"Teach me." I said when I was finally standing before him.

"Teach you what?" His tongue swept over his lower lip, purposely, and I wanted to bite it.

"How to box."

He laughed. "Again?"

"I'm serious this time. No sex. Just teach me how to throw a right hook."

Destry searched my face and then gave me a half smile. "I'm left handed so it's gonna be weird but I'll try."

"Okay."

"A hook is a semi-circular punch thrown with the lead hand, in your case, the right." He moved to stand behind me, positioning my arms with my left one defensively held up in front of my face, then pulled my right arm back, my elbow raised. "In the guard position, which you're in, you draw your elbow back, knuckles forward," he shook my left elbow, "keep your guard hand tucked against your jaw. Always protect your chin." His hands slid down my hips, firmly and then twisted them. "Rotate your hips and torso and then propel your fist through the air in an arc connecting with your opponent."

I was panting by the time he was done telling me all that because his verbal instructions always got me.

Destry stepped back letting go of me. "Come on, let's workout."

I turned and placed my hands on my hips. "What's the matter, too much for you?"

He gave me a challenging stare and stepped toward me, his head burying in my neck. His lips ghosted across my skin sending a shiver through my body. His fingertips dug into my hip bones. "It's not too much, unless you want me to fuck you against these ropes."

Believe me when I say I wanted to. I did. But once that started, I was one step deeper in this whatever we had here. It was going to do nothing more than make it harder when these six weeks were over.

As I started in with the weights, I noticed a difference in a weight I chose. Where it once seemed heavy to lift the ten pound barbells, they seemed light now.

During the workout, Destry looked tired, it wasn't necessarily a physical exhaustion but more like a mental one. Despite our earlier teasing, he wasn't firing on all cylinders right now.

"What'd you do today?"

"Had to help Danny. Fuckin' guy's a mess. Trying to get him straight."

"Why do you have to help him?"

"He's the only family I have, Tallan." The way he said that struck me as odd. Like he was assuming I wouldn't understand if he explained. His eyes dropped to the weights in my hands. "Look at you, tough girl."

I laughed continuing my reps. "I know. Never thought I'd be in shape."

His eyebrow lifted. "Still doing it for him?"

"I don't think I've been doing it for him for a while now."

Destry nodded, his eyes on my form.

"I think that first full mile I ran made me realize that this was about me and changing me *for me* before I could ever consider changing me for someone else." I said that with the confidence of a woman who had stepped out of her comfort zone and met it head on.

Destry just smiled. I know he knew what I was talking about.

We worked out in silence for a bit longer when I'd just finished my second set of chin-ups and asked, "Have you ever lied to anyone, Destry?"

Destry was in the middle of doing a set of chin-ups as well. He'd been participating in exercising for the last week right along side me. I watched his arms as he pulled himself up and down, his shorts hanging low enough on his hips that I could see the muscles in his hips when he lifted himself up. Letting go of the bar, he jumped down on the mat. "I suppose I have. I think I lied to my dad once."

"About what?" Destry didn't strike me as the type of guy who would lie about anything. Or needed to. He was brutally honest at times.

"I went to a party with a friend he told me to stay away from."

"And then what happened?"

"Well, I went, got head, then left." He chuckled rubbing his stomach.

"That's... honest." I couldn't help but laugh.

Destry shrugged, finding it hard to keep a straight face, jumping up on the bar to do another set of chin-ups. "You asked."

"And she's part of the five?"

That made him chuckle again. "Six."

"But you said Stella and four others." Had I got that wrong?

He raised an eyebrow.

Then it finally dawned on me what he meant. "Oh... uh... me. I would make six."

Destry smiled. "Have you?"

"Have I what?"

"Lied." He finished with his third set and jumped down on the mat again.

"Yeah."

"When?"

I shrugged. This wasn't where I wanted the conversation to go. Destry made me nervous. I did my set as he watched, then winked at me.

"You can finally do those with good form."

"I feel great." I said with a deep breath. "These workouts are really helping."

Destry grinned raising his hands over his head and clasped them behind his head. "Maybe it's the after-hours conditioning."

I looked at him from head to toe. "Mmm... could very well be."

He smiled, again, and moved toward the bench press. Hesitating before lying down, he looked over at me. "Are you doing that guy you live with?" he asked, changing the subject, his forehead creased in deep concentration.

"Jared?"

He nodded and then laid down taking a firm grip on the bar.

Standing beside the bench, I watched as he lifted it up and then began a series of reps. "No way. We're just friends. He's doing my best friend anyway and that would just make it *very* weird." And then I asked, "Are you dating anyone?"

He finished the set and then replaced the bar and sat up, his palms flat against the bench. Staring down at his feet, he answered quietly. "I suppose I'm not dating anyone in the sense that I was referring to."

Oh God, what if I'm not the only one he's sleeping with? How come I've never considered that until now?

"And this Silas guy... you loved him?"

"I did, back then. I wasn't lying when I said we'd dated in high school. Then he left and I hadn't heard from him until a few weeks ago."

Again, he only nodded and laid back down for another set.

"Did you love Stella?"

It was a few minutes before he answered. For a moment I thought he wasn't going to. "I did. Very much so."

"Have you thought about talking to her and seeing if you could make it work?"

Stupid idea. Never talk to her again.

His shoulders tensed as he sat back up again. "No. We're done." He stood then and gave me a nod to sit down. He took the majority of the weight off so I could actually lift it.

Just when I thought he'd turn away, maybe I'd asked too much, too private, he surprised me. As I laid down on the bench he straddled the bench, keeping his weight off of me and then placed his hands on the bar hovering over me. He leaned in slowly but just before his lips met mine, he whispered, "I don't want *her*."

If my heart could have melted, it did right then.

It's strange to me that Destry was a total dick when I met him, and now there's this side of him. It's easy to see why he was that way. He was protecting himself.

When the workout was finished, he tilted his head toward the door. "I gotta get going, sorry."

Please don't be meeting another girl!

"Oh, yeah… uh, me too." I reached for my bag on the floor.

"I gotta meet someone tonight but I'll see you tomorrow, right?" He started walking toward the door and then stopped when I didn't follow.

"You go ahead. I'm just gonna stretch and then head out."

I sat there staring at the wall after I got my shoes on. My mind was all over the place jumping from Destry back to Silas again, and then back to Destry and what he was doing to me.

And where he was?

Why did I even care?

Tuesday
May 3, 2011

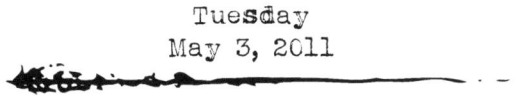

We skipped a workout on Sunday so we made up for it on Tuesday night. Usually Tuesday and Wednesday I didn't work out and it did throw my schedule off a little. I had three articles for the *Seattle Times* to get finished this week but when I was lying awake all night or researching Destry, I had very little time for anything else.

"You wanna go get some food?" he asked as I was changing after our run. "I'm starving."

"Oh, uh, well I already ate. Every Tuesday Jared and I have tacos."

He shrugged reaching for his bag and turned to leave, as if this was no big deal to him. "That's cool."

I reached out and touched his back, stopping him. "But I did work up an appetite."

"If it's the sort of appetite I'm thinking of, there won't be any food involved." He grinned like a kid in a candy store. I love it when he lets all of his defenses down like he was doing now.

"I need food…anything past that won't happen without feeding me!" I laughed on my way out of the basement.

We ended up going to Shiro's Sushi on 2nd street. I loved that place even though it cost me an entire week's salary to go there.

As we ate, Destry looked restless again. As if something was bothering him, but he didn't seem like he wanted to talk about it. I wanted to take away his pain and his burdens. I wanted to help him.

"How's your dad doing?" The thought of James made me smile. I knew I shouldn't have gone to see him but I didn't regret it.

"He's about the same." His eyes fell to the table, chop sticks in his hand. He stirred the soy sauce around mixing it with the wasabi. "He doesn't remember me. And my fucking uncle… he's draining me. I can't keep taking care of him and still look out for myself." Right now, with that vulnerability laced in his words, I could understand why it was so hard for him to be around most people. Why he wore that constant state of anger like a coat of arms. He always had to worry about people's intentions and whether or not they were pure. That didn't exactly make me feel warm and fuzzy.

Right then was when I wanted to quit writing that article and tell Marcus again that I couldn't finish. I knew he would immediately assume my intentions weren't pure. Nothing was farther from the truth.

But if I didn't get this side of Destry captured in that article, people would always have this perception of who they think he is, not who he *really* is. I think the misconception was displayed mostly in the articles about him. Which was where I wanted to make the difference and show him in a different light.

Sometimes I wondered how a man like him could doubt anything. No matter what he said though, he believed that inside the ring, he was the greatest despite losing that fight. I watched a video last night of him that explained his thoughts after the fight.

He was quoted saying, "So what? I lost. He's the better fighter. Big deal."

The thing was, it was a big deal to him. I could tell. He wanted people watching to believe his words. At least that was my theory.

Just when I was about to say something, anything, he placed his napkin on the table, his voice turned serious again. "Back to my place?"

We went back to his apartment and didn't even wait to get inside the door before we had sex. Did it against his door first and then moved to the kitchen. I thought Destry was rough before but have you ever had sex for two hours straight without stopping?

He had me bending in directions I didn't think was humanly possible.

You know you've had good sex when you have a fan on you and you drink a gallon of water in the span of an hour afterwards. His sheets were soaked from sweat. I mean, fuck, it was insane. As gross as sex sweaty sheets sound, it was totally worth it.

I'd just gotten to sleep, sadly in my own bed, but it was the type of sleep where I could have easily been woken up.

And I was. By the rattling of our front door.

Never did I think Jared was serious when he said we had shady neighbors. I mean, I'm not naïve but I didn't think someone would break into our apartment with Jared here. Everyone knew he was a cop. Are they that stupid?

There was more banging around and my heart started to pound. My entire body pricked with a coldness, my eyes frantically searching darkness. What time was it and where was Jared?

I was so sore at that point I actually contemplated just lying there and pulling my blankets over my head. If I couldn't see them, they couldn't see me type of deal.

What do I do? Run? Run where?

They got the door open and that finally woke Jared up. I heard him rustling around in his room after he fell out of bed, probably searching for his gun.

There was an uproar of noise, both from the robber, and Jared, and it was probably just some kid because one look at Jared and his gun and the person bolted.

"That's right, asshole!" Jared yelled.

When I came around the corner holding my unplugged lamp in my hand I was met with Jared's white ass as he stood in the hallway stark naked.

He screamed like a goddamn girl when I tapped on his shoulder. He spun around pointing his gun in my face. "Tallan? Jesus! I'm naked! I could have shot you."

I pushed the gun away. "I see that. And that gun is loaded dumb shit." I smiled and brushed my hair from my face setting my lamp on the floor. My eyes drifted south between his legs. "Hello, old friend."

"The safety is on." Jared shook his head, covering his crotch with his left hand, but still smiled. Scratching the side of his head with the barrel of the gun, he drew in a deep breath trying to calm his nerves.

I motioned to his crotch, and then the gun. "I'm curious. What were you going to do, sword fight him or shoot him?"

He wasn't amused and turned to walk into his bedroom to put clothes on.

I went and closed the front door, locked it, and then for good measure moved the bookcase beside the door in front of it. We were both pretty jumpy after that.

"Should we call the police?" I asked as we cuddled on the couch. I refused to allow any space between us.

"Hello?" He raised an eyebrow at me. "What am I?"

"A patrol cop."

"Doesn't mean I can't handle this." This time Jared shifted to look at me. "And I'm a cop. Just because I'm assigned to patrol right now doesn't mean I'm not a real cop."

"Okay." I held up my palms. "My bad."

"Damn straight, woman." He snorted, turning back around and facing the television. We were watching SpongeBob.

When he turned around, that's when I noticed his shoulder had a large gash on it. "Jared, you're bleeding!"

I don't like the sight of blood. At all. Instantly I felt nauseous.

"How'd that happen?"

"Actually?" His face went pale, almost disgusted.

"I asked, didn't I?"

He groaned running his hands over his face. "That happened at work today. I tried to be nice to this lady crossing the street and she fucking stabbed me."

I covered my mouth, shocked. "Did you arrest her?"

"No." Jared rolled his eyes, pouting a little. "I was screaming in pain. She fucking stabbed me. Her fucking cane doubled as a ninja sword!"

I started laughing so hard I couldn't breathe and then I was reminded of my evening and moaned in pain.

"Rough night?" He mocked, not really caring if I was in pain. Especially not after being stabbed.

"Yeah, I'm really sore."

"From working out?"

"Well, no. I had sex with Destry for like two hours this morning."

Jared's eyebrows drew together. "Two hours? Is that even possible and not cramp up?"

"Apparently so. We did."

He gave me another pouty face, his bottom lip stuck out. "I'm jealous."

"Why? You're sleeping with Catie."

"I haven't in weeks." Jared looked up from the blanket he'd been fidgeting with for the last few minutes but didn't focus on anything in particular. "She's in a relationship with someone she works with."

"What? No way. She never said anything to me about it."

"Did you think she would?"

"Well, yeah. We're friends."

He brought his hands up to his face, ran them through his hair, and then brought them back to his face where they stayed for a moment. He sighed harshly. "Nah, she wouldn't. She knows we're good friends."

I had to pee so I got up and changed into my yoga pants and a hoodie instead of my shorts and tank top and then grabbed my cell phone from my nightstand. There was a text message from a number I didn't recognize.

Tallan it's me Silas. Wanted to make sure you got the ticket.

I didn't reply but I took my phone with me back into the living room and sat down next to Jared. He'd poured himself a bowl of cereal.

"Silas sent me a text." Jared raised an eyebrow but continued eating his cereal. "I thought I wouldn't care as much but for some reason I'm excited to see him. A little."

"It's because you never got over him." He said, then shoved another bite of cereal. When he was done chewing, he added, "First loves are that way."

"And who was your first love?"

Jared smiled, milk dripping on his chin. "Becky Thompson. She pushed me off the big toy when I was eight."

"And you still think about her?"

"I do." He admitted.

"You're a cop. Track her down."

"Don't need to." He finished his last bite of cereal and then drank the milk that remained in the bowl. "She lives next door to my parents. She's married and has two little boys now."

"Wow."

He gave me that look and sighed. "That wasn't the point of my story, Tallan. What I meant was if I had the chance to talk to her, I would."

"So you get it?"

"I've always understood why you wanted to see him. What I didn't get was changing who you are to do so."

He had a point. There was a good part of me that understood I wasn't doing this for Silas anymore. It was about me. It didn't stop the fact that I had to know why Silas left. A girl like me needed the answer to that why. I had to have an answer.

"Have you told Destry?" Jared gave me that look. The fatherly one he had every now and then.

"About Silas?"

"About the article."

"No."

"If you want whatever this is to be something, tell him. The longer you wait, the harder it's going to be to tell him."

There was a sadness to Jared's tone right then. I think he felt more for Catie than he led on. I'd been so wrapped up in my own Silas/Destry troubles that I hadn't even noticed Catie wasn't hanging around much. I'd have to tackle this conversation with Jared when I knew what in the hell I was going to do about my own relationship problems.

Chapter Twelve
HOOK

A hook is an inside power punch. It's a short sideways punch delivered with the elbow bent so the arm forms sort of a hook. The temple, side of the jaw, ribs and liver is the target.

Thursday
May 5, 2011

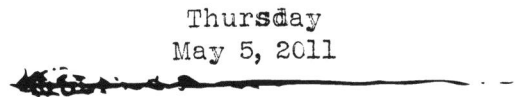

In four weeks, I'd lost fifteen pounds. Destry was good. I can't say it was all from working out, my newfound sexual life had something to do with it.

I was in the basement with Destry, beaming over my results and the new yoga pants and tank top I was wearing. "I can't believe I've lost fifteen pounds already!"

"You look good." He winked picking up a weight from the mat where we were just doing lunges.

"So I didn't before?"

Why did you just ask that? What the hell?

He raised an eyebrow at me. "No, I didn't say that. I would have fucked you even if you hadn't lost anything. You looked good. You looked healthy."

"You say that now but when we first met, you hated me."

"So? That doesn't mean I wouldn't have sex with you. And I did. A few times now."

"So you did hate me?"

"No. I didn't. I don't. But I wasn't friendly and I know that. Sorry. You have to understand that everyone in my life has screwed me over."

My heart started pounding in my chest, pulsing in my ears. "Besides my dad. Don't you think anyone in their right mind would be a little apprehensive to meet someone?"

"Point taken."

Fuck, Tallan. Tell him about the article. Tell him now before you're in too deep. The problem was, it was already too late. It was too late the minute I had sex with him. It was too late the moment I agreed to do the article. I should have asked him first.

"Good." He nodded toward the wall. "Time for squats. So get to them and I'll sit over here and imagine those beautiful thighs wrapped around me."

And I was supposed to somehow concentrate on my form with that visual in my brain? Way to go, Destry.

Thursday
May 12, 2011

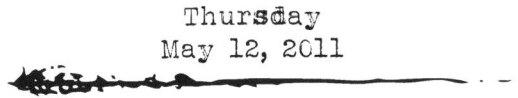

A week passed and I still hadn't told him. A week. But really, I've had five weeks and I hadn't told him. I had the plan that I would finish the article, show it to him, and then ask his permission before giving it to Marcus. That way, if he was upset, I wouldn't publish it.

There comes a point when you know you're past the point of no return. That point was weeks ago but it became even more apparent when Adam, Destry's trainer, spoke to me for the first time. Usually he gave me a nod, nothing else. Didn't even say hello.

Destry knows that I'm a freelance writer. He's never asked much more than that. So it was a little strange having Adam ask me questions like this.

"What kind of articles do you write?" he asked, looking away from me to his left at Destry standing near the wall talking on his cell phone.

I'm a writer. I look for details where others wouldn't. I pick up on questions and how and why they're asked. That's just me.

"Everything from politics to cosmetics." I answered knowing damn well he would sense my apprehension. Fuck. You're screwed, Tallan.

He nodded, his eyes on Destry, and then he looked at me, eyes accessing. "Sports?"

"I do write sports."

I'm dead. I'm fucking dead. He knows.

"Does he know that?"

"No." I admitted taking a deep breath. I'm fucked.

"You better tell him."

"I'm all he has left." Adam gave a nod to Destry. "Everyone else has fucked him over, including his manager. Don't add your name to that list because once you're on it with him, you'll never get off it." He walked past me without another word.

I couldn't just blurt this out. It would take some time to explain to Destry.

When I looked at Destry, his mood seemed off but he smiled. I felt like his mood had something to do with Adam. Maybe he already told him. But did I have the guts to say anything to him that night?

No. I was scared of him. If he was in a bad mood, I didn't want to make it worse. If he was in a good mood, I didn't want to ruin it.

The thing was, I believed wholeheartedly that I could make a difference for Destry. The world had an image of him and it was the wrong one. Hell, I had an image of him when I first met him and it wasn't anything like what my initial assessment was now. Maybe it was my way of justifying my indiscretions, maybe not.

Not a lot was said between us that night. His mood was definitely off. Sidelong looks sent my way that didn't quite meet his eyes, just glances. I couldn't distinguish from my own paranoia about keeping the article a secret and if there was something more personal going on with Destry. His eyes were the giveaway, a lack of emotion as he looked at me on and off all night.

Maybe he had some shit going on with his dad he didn't want to talk about. I don't know but his mood change threw me off. Adam's remarks were also the fuel to my paranoid fire. I felt like I was working out and was the only one in the room. Not much was said, and in that silence, the message I was getting was loud and clear.

After our workout, we parted ways and not a lot was said. That night I sat down and decided I was going to finish the article. Maybe I wouldn't submit it, but I had to finish it. Around midnight, I got a text from Destry.

Come over?

Here's the thing. The shitty thing if you asked me. I could have told him that night. I should have. I didn't because I wanted what this was for as long as I could have it. I knew once he knew, it was over.

I went to him though. It took me around twenty minutes to get over to his apartment. When I did, he smiled, his mood still tense and gave a nod into his apartment. I walked past him and stood in the kitchen, waiting for him after setting my bag on the counter.

The door slammed, startling me. And then I was being lifted off the ground. My legs wrapped around him on instinct. There wasn't a lot of words said and I understood there wouldn't be tonight. He needed something and I was going to give him what he needed. In fact, nothing was said.

His lips crashed into mine, warm, relentless and unyielding and so fucking perfect. I matched him with everything I had, wanting everything he was going to give me. Laid on the center of his bed, hovering over me, he took a shaky breath and moaned into my mouth pressing his weight into me. It felt like the first breath he had taken since we got in here, labored and needy. His hand slipped from my cheek and down the valley between my breasts, eyes remaining locked with mine.

Without saying anything, I brought his mouth back to mine wanting more of those intense kisses. They were so different and consuming, I had to have them.

This time was slow, every movement was in slow motion, each one thought out and deliberate. Our breathing was low, but ragged, our movements dawdling but extremely passionate. Our kisses, deep, but tender.

Something threw me about his motions. Like this was some sort of a goodbye?

Why would he be this gentle with me? This isn't us. We're rough. We fuck. We don't do gentle.

My eyes went to his, only he wasn't looking at me. Instead his eyes were closed, his left hand was behind the nape of my neck, his right resting against my thigh he wrapped around his waist, and then he began to move a little faster. Never breaking his steely gaze from mine, my lips moved from his to kiss his shoulders, memorizing how the muscles felt against the sensitive skin of my lips. His warm breath washed over me, overriding any coherent thought I had. He looked down at me, and I gasped. There was some concentration in his features, sure, but there was something more there that I couldn't place.

With the way this felt, I never wanted it to end. I was finally feeling what I was meant to feel. This was so completely different from anything we'd experienced before. His hands that were wrapped around my waist moved to my ass, fisting the flesh in his strong hands and driving into me a little harder than before. His mouth, hot and heavy, moved from my neck and found my lips. His left hand reached down and adjusted my leg allowing him to go deeper, exactly where I needed him as his mouth tenderly sought out mine. The kissing was unreal. So much emotion, hurt and need brought forth with it.

What the hell did all this mean? I was so confused.

It didn't take long before our desire gave way, and our movements were driven. Destry's hand was still wrapped around the back of my neck, his fingers digging into my skin. His right hand was on my hip, securing me to him as his movements sped. A handful of thrusts later, his body jerked in time with his release, his head buried in my shoulder groaning, his hands on my ass cheeks squeezing harder.

He collapsed his entire weight on me, his breath hot and rapid on my neck as he panted. I let my hands that were on his shoulders fall away to the mattress, my own breathing just as rough.

I lifted slightly so he could remove his hands from under me. He did and sighed heavily, gasping as if he couldn't catch his breath. That's when the weariness settled over us, and he rolled to the side away from me. Pushing himself up onto his elbows, he hesitated and then looked over at me, he gave me a tentative but uneasy smile.

"Sleep well," he breathed, parting his lips over mine.

Brushing the side of his face against my hair, his nose ran along my ear. Staring at each other like this, I could see this being my future, our future, but this cloud hanging over us… *over me*… was this unspoken burden that couldn't be voiced without serious repercussions. Not only the burden of the article but merely the burden of me seeing Silas in a few days was hanging like a thundercloud over this place, over us, and left me in a state of flux, leaning one way one minute and wanting to spill my guts and tell him everything and another way another minute with the silence I kept to myself like an imaginary friend I couldn't tell anyone about.

Destry continued to focus on me as my eyes slowly drifted, the physical and emotional baggage becoming almost too much to bear for me.

As I drifted closer to sleep, right now I saw it in his eyes, in his touch, he felt something more than sex but he was holding back. Maybe this was even his way of letting go.

Friday
May 13, 2011

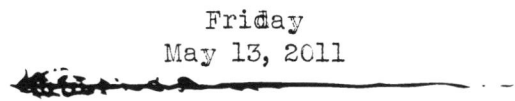

I stayed with him that night, his arms wrapped around me. When I woke up around four, my back was pressed to his chest, his breathing light. I turned my head with one eye open to see that he was still sleeping.

I laid awake for probably an hour wondering what that was that we did a few hours ago. It was so completely different than what we had ever done before.

Destry's bedroom window was open, the steady rain that fell created a hissing sound as cars passed by.

As careful as I could I removed myself from the bed.

When I got outside his apartment the spring morning was cool, a thick cloud cover and a gentle breeze blew over the city bringing with it the salty ocean smell. The rain had let up, the streets still streaming with water. My feet drug on the pavement as I trudged my way up the hill to my apartment. I felt like I hadn't slept in days, a heaviness rooting my steps.

When I got back to my apartment I opened my lap top and finished the article and I have to say it felt good. My hands were literally shaking when I finished it because I knew what it meant.

```
The Trainer by Tallan Spencer
Did Destry Stone throw the fight?
That's the question on everyone's minds these days.
He's said to be the biggest upset in heavyweight history.
They say he walked away at the first knock out.
A lot of people want to know more about the man who shuns
the media.
Who is he?
He's the only child of heavyweight champion boxer James Stone.
Born in Boise, Idaho, he moved to Seattle with his father in
1998 when his parents split up. He grew up shadowing his
father in the basement of his uncle's bar.
His father, James, describes Destry as a happy boy, but with
something to prove. "He told me when he was three he'd be a
champion of the world. I believed him. He was the greatest
part of my life."
It's no question that Destry is described as an angry child,
always getting in fights.
I've personally heard people say he's always so aggressive.
But why?
"He's always been that way from what I could gather. So full
of hate and no one knows why." Said his uncle as he leans
into the bar, his eyes distant and far away. "That boy has
been through more than any kid should have to."
Having grown up in a ring, it was no surprise this boxer
prodigy would find his way into the professional boxing
association. At only eighteen years of age, he fought in his
```

first sanctioned fight as a heavyweight boxer on November 11, 2004, winning with a second round knock-out. Two years later, on his twentieth birthday, he fought Stefan Aksakov in Japan with a third round knock out to become the WBO World Heavyweight Champion. He'd hold the title for four years, still undefeated with an impressive, if not unheard of, knockout record until December 18, 2010, shortly after his twenty-fourth birthday, when he went down in the fifth round by knock-out in the fight against Ray Lucas.

So was the fight fixed?

That question is not easily answered.

I met Destry when I decided I needed to get in my own fighting shape. And while he wasn't the nicest person, he helped me. From the first moment I met him, I knew there was something more. What you notice first is that guard he has, never letting himself feel too much. The second, the scowl, like he's trying to figure you out.

Only spend five minutes around the guy and his eyes tend to give him away. At first, I didn't see that. I saw the arrogance he displayed. What I did see was a man who had been used. What I saw was a man who was so much more than the gloves he wore.

These days you can find Destry in the basement of that same bar his father trained at. What is he training for?

After all he lost the title, right?

"I'm training for a fight I know I'll win."

So that leaves many to speculate what fight is he referring to? Although he was obtuse about why he still trained every day, he did insinuate that what poople's perceptions of how that fight went down will change in the near future. "People have no idea what was going through my mind that night... until you walk in my shoes, you just cannot understand." Stone said staring at the brick wall in the basement with a poster of his father holding a championship belt.

So can we expect this redemption of a man wronged? Destry was pretty mum on any details only saying that, "time was definitely on his side and all will be made right."

I, for one, cannot wait to see how this plays out and based on

the times I witnessed him training in his basement gym, he's
in it to win it...whatever that means.

It took me the better part of the day before I tweaked the article,
added some more details to it so that I was satisfied with the article on
Destry.

If he read it, he'd understand and I could make him see why. We
agreed to meet at six that night. Destry said he had something to do
tonight, but didn't say what.

When I got there, he was in front of a black punching bag throwing
jabs, hooks and uppercuts, his eyes trained intently on the bag. Each
hit was more powerful than the next as Nine Inch Nails blared in the
background.

My moves were hesitant as I approached the far wall where I usually
left my bag on most days. As I rounded the corner, that's when I saw
Adam standing ten feet from Destry leaned against the wall watching
him.

Destry was hitting the bag so hard and fast that he had no form.
Just anger. It sent a chill through my blood to see him like that, his
menacing scowl set ahead. He stopped, panting and let his gloved
hands fall to his sides.

"That's enough, bro." Adam said, pushing himself from the wall.

Destry hung his head forward seeming lifeless and defeated, his
gloved hands resting on his hips. His eyes squeezed shut as he nodded,
never looking up.

Adam reached over and patted his back. Nothing was said to him.

After retrieving a bag, Adam approached me next, only my eyes
were focused on Destry. It took me a moment but my stare gained focus
on Adam.

My body froze when he lightly bumped my shoulder and stopped
beside me, never looking at me. "You... should have told him." He
whispered.

My breath caught, my vision blurred when my eyes rose to Destry as he sat down on the weight bench and began unwrapping his gloves. I was humiliated in so many ways, my head pounded, eyes burning as I stared at a man I just might have destroyed.

Adam left, the metal door slamming shut echoing through the room and Destry looked up from his place on the bench.

I froze, unsure of what would happen next. My body trembled with fear.

How did this happen? How did I get so blindsided by thinking I could help him that I forgot to realize by not telling him I was no different than Stella or any other woman who's ever let him down.

I'm a fucking idiot.

I moved on instinct toward him, an apprehensive weight giving me hesitation.

At first, he didn't look up. And then, slowly, he lifted his head and looked at me. There was an uncensored pain there that he wanted me to see. There's no indifference now. Just pain.

It was quite possibly the silence that was my undoing. I think that waiting during the calm before the storm was the worst. The fear of the unknown. What was he going to say or do when we finally talked about this? Would he even talk or just leave me standing here feeling helpless to do anything about this situation that I'd caused?

You could feel the tension rising from him. He didn't make a movement or a sound until I said something. His eyes closed and then he slowly opened them when I spoke.

"Hey."

Hey? That's what you say right then. Tell him. This is your chance.

When our eyes finally met, he sat there and stared at me for a moment. The rush of reality crashed into me right then. With the way he looked at me, he knew. The air changed, I could feel it being sucked from the room. His confused expression caught me, his brow creased as he ran his hand across the back of his neck. He was hesitating. I tasted bile, my skin pricked with needles, my heart sinking.

Say something. Explain. Do something. Our eyes caught again.

Destry was normally so sure of himself, but right now he was none of that. He looked uncertain. Something flickered behind the usual indifference, then he gave me a fleeting look.

"No work out today." His voice was grave and tense as his jaw flexed. He stood, as though he was going to leave.

I wanted to cry, right then, but I didn't deserve the tears. I was so shocked and appalled with myself that I couldn't move. I felt hopeless.

With his back to me, he let out a heavy growling breath, his palms swiped down his face and over his eyes before he spun around to face me, his head lifted arrogantly. "I know about the article." Wanting to see my reaction, he spun around to look at me.

And then he waited for the retaliation of my words, but they didn't come. Trying to hold on to some dignity, I told myself not to cry. It wasn't easy. There was a certain amount of significance behind those words, though I knew they were coming, it rendered me speechless. I was trying to remain calm, but I couldn't help my voice from trembling.

"What?" I asked with a justifiable amount of hesitation.

He swept his trembling hand across the back of his slick neck and then suddenly, his fist slammed into the wall. "Did I fucking stutter?" He was silent again, his body taut and motionless as he stared at me.

I jumped back at the sound his anger caused and fell back against the far wall where my bag was.

Destry closed his eyes, shaking his head, his breathing was heavy and uneven.

"I'm sorry I hurt you." I reached inside my bag for the article I printed. "But if you would just read it—"

He picked up the bar on the bench beside him that had at least two hundred pounds on it, raised it over his head like it weighed nothing and threw it. "Goddamn you! I fucking... I..." he was struggling for words to express how he felt. "Get out! Leave!"

Anger replaced the disbelief in his eyes. There's a wicked side to Destry. I haven't even begun to see it and maybe I didn't want to. It's harsh and I wondered how often others saw this side.

When I didn't move, he shook his head.

"I can't fucking believe you." He said flatly, desperation turning to anger. "*You*, of all people."

"Destry… I'm your friend. If you'd just read it you'd understand."

"Fuck you." He turned to face me, shaking his head. I could see now that his body was shaking. "I never asked for you to be my friend." He started to walk away and then stopped suddenly. "And you can tell that no good piece of shit you work for, the next time I see him, I'm going to not just clock his ass, I'm going to kill him."

I didn't realize how he would perceive that story. I didn't even think that he would imagine I would hurt him like that. He kept his eyes on mine as if he was challenging me to reply. I wasn't going to. I wasn't going to let him know how bad that hurt.

Destry and I hadn't defined our relationship, and I didn't see where we really needed to. Neither did Destry, or so I thought. I still hadn't told him how I felt, though I was sure he knew. I just hadn't said the words out loud. How could he have thought I would do that to him? I think because of my silence, he felt that there were some underhanded reasons for me writing this article. He just has to read it.

"How long have you known?" Timidly I stood there, unsure if I should leave or stay. I knew by the look on his face he wanted me to leave.

"Three days." His gaze was fixed on the ground as he spoke. I felt relieved not to have that stare on me.

"And last night, you knew?" A silence spread over us as I waited for him to answer.

He gave a tip of his head, his anger harsh. "Yep."

"So you slept with me anyway?"

"You were willing. Who was I to deny you?"

As much as I didn't want to admit it, I felt like he used me for his own pleasure. A little taste of the pain I caused him. "You're a bastard."

"Maybe so." He gave a bitter laugh. "But you're the one who used me first." He tore his eyes away from mine and turned to walk away but stopped abruptly. He spun around to look at me before he got to the door, he looked at me with dark eyes, his breathing heavy, his anger slow, silent, but so strong. "Are you still meeting him?"

I said nothing. What the hell would I say right then?

"What are you going to do," he pressed, "So what, are you gonna fuck him and think of me?" he said, his face turning puce with infuriating anger that briefly overpowered the slur.

He really was a cocky bastard, wasn't he?

He stepped closer with nothing more than harsh breathing and silent words for a moment. Wounded green eyes fringed by dark lashes settled on my face, studying me with an unnerving intensity. "Did you, or did you not, write an article about me."

I swallowed but said nothing.

He tipped his head and his hand raised and lifted my chin. "I asked you a fucking question and I expect a goddamn answer. No bullshit."

"Yes. I wrote an article but can you at least let me explain and read it?"

"Get out." He looked like he couldn't breathe and wanted to vomit. I nearly did.

Destry's eyes searched mine as I grasped the meaning behind his words.

"Fine," was my only response, tears streaming down my face. I reached inside my bag and then hauled it over my shoulder, handing him the article and the remaining three hundred I owed him for being my personal trainer.

I was hurt and humiliated, only I knew the reason and I deserved those feelings.

Chapter Thirteen
KNOCKDOWN

A knockdown occurs when a boxer gets hit and touches the floor with any part of his body other than his feet, is being held up by the ropes, or is hanging on, through, or over the ropes and cannot protect himself or fall to the floor.

Saturday
May 14, 2011

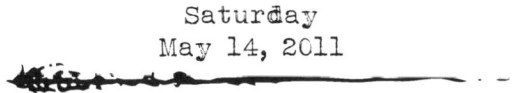

The next morning, I called him, no answer. Nothing. There was an envelope slid under our door with the money I'd given him last night, but no note. Nothing.

I stopped by the bar hoping maybe he'd read the article and would talk to me, only Danny said he hadn't seen him. My heart ached thinking about never seeing him again, never getting him to see what my intentions were behind what I did.

The thing was, you make eye contact with thousands of people every day. Some you remember, others you don't. I would always remember the first time I made eye contact with Destry Stone. He made sure of that. I would remember that stare and the way he squinted when he focused on something. That indifference. That coldness. All of it.

I wanted to run to him and make him listen to me but I knew he wouldn't give me the time of day.

My body ached. I wanted the pain to stop. Hell, at this point, I'd give up my lungs not to feel this pain anymore. I didn't need them anyway. It hurt too bad to breathe.

The truth was, I couldn't and didn't know how I would ever move on from this. It was so much different than what I felt when Silas left, surprisingly. Maybe it was because I was older and my heart had already been broken once, a crack. Now it was splitting in two. A complete break.

When I got back to our apartment, I decided that I was either going to sit in front of the television and cry all day, or bake.

I love to bake. Which would explain how I gain weight so easily. I constantly bake. My favorite?

Peach pie. I make it all year long too. My favorite is in the summer, peach pie, with fresh peaches. Canned ones work too though. I'm not that picky. Baking is my specialty and pretty much the only thing I'm good at.

As I made it, I thought about when I first learned to make pie with my mom when I was seven. She explained in detail every process, from the picking, to the baking. I remember being enthralled in every word she said, knowing someday, I would be doing this very same thing. Only now, as I repeated the steps to myself, I found a little different meaning in the process.

Have you ever watched a peach fall from a tree?

Deep in the heart of summer, so ripe, so pretty, soft, juicy, and delicious, it was ready. The peach lets go, free falls, and maybe it falls into dirt, so rich, so warm, wrapped in the Earth's heart. Or maybe it falls on grass, shiny blades of grass green wrapped in wet, refreshing drops.

The gentle hands that found it decided how it would end up. Peach crisp, pie, cobbler, jam, and any other sugar-sweet or salty treat—it let go and just fell. Fell where it needed to fall.

I wasn't sure how I would end up. Pie, cobbler, jam, or maybe even crisp. But I fell from that tree.

Ready to be made into something.

I had fallen for Destry. I wasn't sure what falling meant but for the first time since I'd been with Silas, my heart was beating that way. I was that peach.

The thought of how badly I hurt Destry like I did was such a consuming feeling that it destroyed me. Deep down, Destry was a nice guy. He was just misunderstood in many ways. This article was something I needed to print. I'd go against his wishes but I didn't need his approval to print it.

There I was elbow deep in peaches and pie crust when Jared walked in and smiled. It was only six in the morning and I was baking.

He set his gun on the counter along with his bullet proof vest as he buttoned his shirt.

"Good morning." I said, never looking up and then showed him my pie. "Peach pie?"

"You know the way to my heart." He laughed.

I stopped what I was doing and gave him a look. One he knew. "If I can't find anyone to marry me by the time I'm thirty, will you?"

Jared smiled and sat down at the kitchen table with a bowl of cereal. "Arranging marriages now?"

"More like back up plans." I put my hands back in the pie crust and took the fork to get the crust the way I wanted it, flat and smooth.

Jared took a bite of his cereal and then looked over at me. "I don't want to be a backup plan."

"Would you marry me?"

The look on his face, the one of amusement said a lot. "Are you asking me?"

"No."

He turned back to his bowl and the paper now in his hand. "Well, there's your answer."

When the crust was ready, I put it in the oven to brown it and then took my bowl of peaches and cinnamon over to the table. "Jared, why does this shit always happen to me?"

"Because."

I fisted the peaches in my hands. "This is what I feel like!"

He raised an eyebrow. "Say what?"

"Nothing."

Jared stared at me trying to understand how my situation was related to peaches. "Did you really see this going differently?"

"No." I sighed leaning my head against the wall. "Deep down, I knew."

"Then what's the problem?"

It took me a moment but then I spilled my guts to my best friend. "I'm frustrated. I had this plan. I had a plan for a lot of things in life and nothing has ever turned out the way I wanted."

Jared, as usual, wasted no time in telling me how it was. "That's something you have to change, Tallan. You want to write for magazines instead of blogs and newspapers, but you never submit anything. You've talked about writing a novel, but have you ever made the effort to do so?"

All valid points. I did just enough to get by and when it didn't work out, I thought it was the world's way of letting me know happiness wasn't in my future.

He leaned forward. "You can't control life, Tallan. What you can control is how you live it."

"Fine." I threw a peach at him. It smacked him in the cheek and fell into his lap. "Kick me while I'm down."

Sometimes I think we have this version of love, and life for that matter that doesn't exist. And if it does, most of us never find it. Maybe too scared, we shy away from it. We're too cynical and refuse to see what's right in front of us.

Deep down, we want to laugh nervously, hold sweaty hands, believe in love, be passionate, be fearless but we can't unless we believe it can happen. And let it fall where it is supposed to fall.

Chapter Fourteen
LACING

Pushing with or using the bottom side of an open glove where the laces are to rub the face of an opponent. Lacing can cut the face.

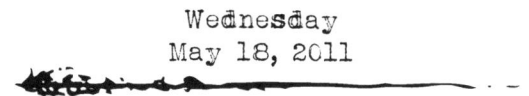

Wednesday
May 18, 2011

Today was the day of the concert. I spent most of the day trying to talk myself out of going but then eventually I thought about what Jared had said. "You can control life. You can control how you live it."

I had just gotten my dress on staring at myself in the mirror when Jared appeared behind me leaning in the door frame still dressed in his uniform.

"Am I going to have to cut you out of it?"

"You tell me." I turned to face him, my hands smoothing down the side of the dress.

"I lost a lot more than weight the past six weeks…weight I may or may not put back on but losing Destry, I'm afraid, was forever." I said as my eyes started to well up.

Jared sighed. "It's a shame we never worked out."

"Such a shame." I agreed with a laugh as I swiped at my eyes, trying not to ruin my makeup.

Jared stepped forward. He was naturally protective and had been since I'd met him. He never met Silas but rock star didn't exactly give him the vibe he wanted.

I really didn't think Jared had anything to worry about. Then again, I didn't know Silas anymore.

"I'm going to be a big brother right now. I don't want you going tonight. I'm not comfortable with you going. Something doesn't feel right."

"Jared." I reached out and touched his cheek. "I'll be fine. I'm just going to talk to him and then I'm leaving. I'm not staying for the concert."

He still seemed uneasy, but asked, "Have you heard from Destry?"

"Nope. He left the money I paid him under the door and he's basically disappeared."

"Yikes."

I stepped around Jared and down the hall, he followed. "He'll never forgive me."

"Did you give the article to Marcus?"

"Not yet. I told him I wasn't ready to submit it yet."

When I reached for my purse, Jared sighed again, his uneasy features evident. "Call me if you need me."

I forced myself to breathe evenly. "I will."

He didn't leave right away, he couldn't. Jared was scared.

"Go ahead, tell me I'm an idiot."

He gave a slight smile and opened the door. "You're an idiot."

"Thank you."

When I stepped out the door and waited for a cab, that's when the reality of what I was about to do hit me.

I loved Silas more than anything when I was eighteen. Five years later, my heart still held a place for him. I didn't know what that place was, but it was there. Almost like a void.

When I agreed to meet him, I thought maybe this one night could be what my life was missing. Help me move on and give myself a chance at finding happiness. If that happiness was with Silas, I was okay with that. Well, I was okay with that was six weeks ago. Now, I wasn't as sure.

What I didn't see was that I hadn't been looking for love. I wasn't even giving it a chance. It wasn't because I was caught up on Silas and what he did to me. It was like I couldn't move on without an answer.

I couldn't tell you why I hadn't moved on from Silas but it was more than likely because I didn't understand why he left.

Then I met Destry Stone. And everything changed completely.

I still had to have that answer though.

When Silas left I never got an answer as to why—a question that a girl like me, the one looking for the story, the underlining meaning, needed. And I'd admit, part of me, the story seeker, had thought maybe after all this time I would finally get my answer.

Some would wonder if I had moved on. Most would hope, right? Especially after everything with Destry. Unfortunately for me, that hadn't happened. I might have physically moved on, but there was a good part of me that, after seeing him, still hoped I would get the answer.

Chapter Fifteen
POWER PUNCHES

Power punches are hooks, straight rights or lefts, uppercuts, or stiff jabs.
Power punches are solid punches to the chin, head, or body that inflict
damage.

I didn't take into account the traffic getting to the concert. Strangely enough this was the first time Silas Cade had returned to Seattle for a concert. Everyone wanted to see him because of that. Hometown famous rock star returns home.

Last night Silas told me to meet his assistant at the entrance and she would take me back.

By the time I got to the Key Arena, the opening band was already on.

Rachel, the assistant he told me about, was there waiting for me when I arrived. With a smile that struck me as fake, she handed me a pass I placed around my neck. "You're Tallan Spencer, right?" I nodded. "You're late."

"Nice to meet you."

Isn't she just pleasant as all hell?

She gave a nod, waving at me but never offering her hand. "I'm Rachel Mattis. I'm Mr. Cade's assistant."

Mr. Cade? How formal.

I took one look at her twelve-year-old body and knew Silas had probably slept with her. She was that typical bony super-model thin I constantly saw hanging off him in photographs.

Rachel took me through doors, down a long hallway and through two more sets of doors. Around us equipment was scattered, people talked to men in ripped jeans hanging on barely legal woman with half their ass hanging out. It was definitely a rock concert. I felt completely out of place. A man to my right was staring at me, his black ripped t-shirt hanging off him and a tattoo on his face. Classy.

When I looked at him, he gave me a once over and then winked.

My attention went to Rachel when she knocked on a door. My heart was in my throat, my hands shaking when I realized the person behind that door was Silas. I had second thoughts right then.

Rachel gave me a nod and then pushed the door open. My feet would barely move.

When I did walk in, Silas was there with his feet up on the table in front of him staring at his cell phone in his right hand. In the left was a glass filled with a honey colored liquid over ice. My heart pounded but this wasn't the feeling I thought I would feel.

He looked up immediately and blinked. Slowly he took in my appearance. My hair was longer, my hips wider, maybe even a few wrinkles since the last time he saw me. I wasn't that eighteen-year-old girl anymore.

With head to toe tattoos. Silas looked very different from the boy I knew in high school. He had filled out, fit, but had nothing on Destry when it came to muscles.

His dark hair was messy but artfully spiked in the front. He watched me curiously as I stepped inside the room, his brow slightly scrunched. "Tallan?"

"Yeah?" I finally met his eyes. Same blue.

I wanted green.

He shook his head, a soft smile gracing his full lips. My eyes went to the lip ring I hadn't seen in photographs. It suited him well. "You're just as beautiful as I remember."

Cheesy. Stupid. Leave now. That's what I told myself.

I'll be honest, I didn't plan on staying that night. I even told Jared I wouldn't. I would meet up with him only because I needed to know. I was no longer interested in anything else. What Silas and I had back then was lost. It was lost the day he walked away with no answer. I truly wished him happiness, but I wasn't his happiness any longer. I knew that now looking at him. It wasn't there.

Nothing he said tonight could change that. Destry had opened my eyes to what I refused to see these last five years. Just because one star goes out doesn't mean another isn't lit for you. Doesn't mean you can't blow it out either.

I wanted an answer so I just came out with it.

"Why?" I asked refusing to waste any time.

"I don't blame you for hating me." He stood, his body tensed as he held up his palms. "I expected it. I deserve it."

Rachel stuck her head in. "It's time."

She disappeared and Silas walked toward the door.

"Really? Why am I here, Silas?" He had no idea how much he deserved my anger. I looked back so furiously hurt I was scared my voice would break and I wouldn't get out what I needed. "You expected it? Deserved it? Fucking right you did. I loved you, Silas. And not just any love. I was ready to marry you, forget everything I ever wanted, for you. It was the half of myself, fucking holding my ripped out heart in my hands type of love!"

"Just please stay and we can talk about this after. I have to get out there." He begged, sounding like he was ready to drop to his knees as he walked towards the door. "Just please stay. I have to get out there but don't leave. I want to talk to you after the concert. Please."

I hoped he did fall to his knees because maybe, just maybe, he would feel that pain I had felt for so long. The pain that had consumed me longer than I wanted to remember.

I started a different walk of shame out of this place, leaving Silas just like he'd left me all those years ago.

"Why?" I asked following him despite my lack of visibility between the tears of anger at this man who had consumed my past. In the distance, to the right, I could see the stage lights and the howl of the crowd shouting his name.

"Because I want to talk to you after the show. I can't right now," Silas said, like it was that easy. Like I should listen to him no matter what. He had now almost reached me, as our heavy steps were silenced by a pounding of the fans.

"I should go."

"Why can't I explain?" He sounded frustrated. I was too. "I gave you that ticket. Why can't you just stay?"

My stomach lurched, twisting into more anger and resentment as about ten people swarmed around him, another two bodyguards flanking his sides. "Why should you be able to explain, Silas? You could have explained before leaving me years ago."

Silas groaned almost seeming sincere. "Because I'm sorry. I *never* meant to hurt you, Tallan." He kept apologizing and repeating himself as he walked away toward the stage, but still, I didn't have the answer I was looking for.

He turned around then, his tall frame disappearing on stage. I could no longer see him, but I could hear him take the stage.

"Seattle!" He shouted in the microphone. "How's my hometown?"

I should go. I told myself to go. But then I'd never get my answer.

Chapter Sixteen
BELOW THE BELT

Below the belt is an imaginary line from the belly button to the top of the hips where a boxer is not supposed to hit. To hit below the belt is to not behave according to the rules of decency.

I honestly couldn't tell you anything about that concert other than the very first song he played was "Never Knew" and he dedicated it to me. Silas played for two hours and I watched him from the front row. But I heard nothing but that first song. My mind was elsewhere. I thought of Destry the entire time. I wasn't sure I meant a goddamn thing to him anymore, but he sparked something inside of me that made me want more. Deserve more. I wanted to have just an ounce of the passion he had for fighting.

The only reason I stayed for that concert was to get my answer.

After the concert he asked me to go to Q Nightclub with him. I'm an idiot because I went. I thought somehow we'd be able to finally talk away from the crowds and groupies.

"Why now, Silas?" I asked when we were tucked away in the back of the nightclub in a private room.

"I missed you." His words were slurred as he slouched in the booth, watching me. There was a distinct difference between the Silas I saw before the concert, and now. He was high, on what, I had no idea. But I still needed my goddamn answer.

"Why did you leave and only offer me a phone call? I thought I meant more to you than that?"

"I was a dumb kid." He looked up when a tall blonde handed him a drink. She set one down for me too. One I had no intention of drinking. "I was… a dick and I'm sorry."

I shook my head crossing my arms over my chest remembering Destry's words. "That's not good enough."

"Then why are you here?" He laughed leaning forward to retrieve his drink. He took a sip and then waited for my answer. "You didn't really think you'd come here and we'd talk, did you?"

Destry was right. Jared was right.

"Because I had to hear you say it in person." I admitted feeling uncomfortable.

I'd gone over it in my head—what I would say to him, the words, the expression, the tone—all of it. This, right now, wasn't how I saw it happening.

"No. You're here because you wanted to see me too."

"Yes, I did. I'll admit when you called I didn't care what happened between us. Just that I got to see you again. I was so hung up on just knowing that you even remembered me, I didn't care how you remembered me. If that makes sense. But I do now. I care. I wanted to know why. Why after five years would you call me?"

He had no answer at first and just about the time I was ready to give up, he answered. "Because I missed you, Tallan. It's not that complicated. And Marcus said... he said you wanted to see me. I thought you know, what the hell for old time's sake."

"Marcus? Wait... what?"

What the fuck is he talking about? Marcus? My Marcus?

"Marcus Hadley. He called me months back and said you wanted to see me and gave me your number."

Silas stood, as though none of this mattered when a slow bass kicked and a song I knew came over the speakers. Two of his body guards watched closely but kept their distance, his hand reached for mine. "Come on baby, dance with me."

He reached down and pulled me up. I pushed back my hands on his shoulders. "No, Silas. You're high."

I had strength—thanks to Destry—but I couldn't hold off Silas. I didn't think he'd do anything stupid but now I understood.

"What do you mean Marcus called you?"

Silas sighed taking a step back. "He called me."

"So..." and then it hit me, the realization of everything came suddenly like a sucker punch to my face, a below the belt hit. "You never *would have* called me if he wouldn't have called you?"

He shrugged rolling his eyes. "Why does it matter?" he leaned in, as if I would kiss him.

"No, answer the question. You wouldn't have called, would you?"

Silas shook his head in annoyance. "No. I wouldn't have... but you're here now. Let's make the best of tonight. Just one night."

Was he fucking serious?

Apparently so.

I'd had Destry show me a move or two in the ring but what I should have had him help me with was self defense. I had no chance against a man who was high right now. His strength amplified by whatever was flowing through his veins.

A nervous sweat was taking me over. I couldn't fight off this guy who had loved me a long time ago. What's worse? He had bodyguards standing guard over more than just the safety of Silas. I was a virtual prisoner with no chance in hell of walking away unscathed, physically and emotionally.

It was then that his body guards moved, based on his nod to them, and I was trapped inside the private room. Absolutely no one would be able to hear me scream, if I did. I had my phone in my purse and dialed when Silas turned his head to reach for his drink, his grip on my waist loosening.

I should have called Jared but he doesn't answer when he's on duty.

I had no idea if Destry would answer, but I had to try at this point.

He answered, surprisingly. I kept my phone on in my purse to let him hear me telling Silas no.

"Silas, just let me leave, please." I said loud enough that I knew Destry would be able to hear. "I want to leave...get your fucking hands off of me!"

"Nah, you should stay. I'll show you a good time. Show you what you've been missing all this time."

I was screwed because despite calling Destry, how the hell was he going to know where I was?

The answer? He wouldn't.

For five minutes I tried to leave but Silas wouldn't let me. There was commotion out on the dance floor, and then around the room.

He came for me. Is he Superman because how the hell did he find me? I wasn't too concerned with that because that's when I knew he followed me tonight. He had to have. There was no other answer for it. Destry's eyes found mine, and there was some uncertainty from both of us. I was nervous. I wasn't sure how he was going to react to me.

Silas didn't see him at first and pulled me against his chest, his eyes so dark you couldn't see the blue in them anymore. "Isn't this what you wanted? Why are you acting like a bitch now? Every girl wants to fuck a rock star."

I pushed back trying to get away from him, knowing Destry was seeing this. "Because I want to leave."

When he faced me, his shoulders squared, jaw rigid, he asked me, though his question was delivered to Silas, "What the fuck is going on?"

"What does it look like is going on?" Silas' bloodshot eyes drifted toward Destry, his arm wrapping around my shoulder and tightened. "We're busy. Leave."

"I see that." Destry's eyes shifted from mine to Silas, cold and indifferent. "But I think the lady wants to leave."

"Says who?" Silas snorted.

"Her." Destry pointed at me. "She called me."

"Bullshit." Silas gave him a look that was more of a warning. I'm sure it worked for most, the ones intimidated by his rock star image. But it would never work for Destry. "She's been with me the entire time."

Destry pointed and raised an eyebrow at me. "Tell him."

I looked at Silas, tears streaming down my face. I was so stupid. "I called him. I want to leave."

"I'm not finished here." Silas reached for my hand grasping my wrist. "You can't leave."

"Excuse me?" Destry asked, raising an eyebrow at Silas.

"You heard me, *champ*." Destry laughed shaking his head. "Get lost."

That was clearly the wrong thing to say to Destry. Even I knew that. He didn't like being referred to as champ and definitely not by Silas.

"I don't think I heard you, rock star. Say it again." Destry shoved Silas, who stood chest to chest with him and reached for my hand.

"Who the fuck do you think you are?" Silas looked to his boys, laughing. "You trying to make a move on my girl?"

My girl? Oh he's certainly high. And delusional.

"She ain't your girl, man. You lost that chance."

Silas' eyes skipped to Destry. His eyes, so dark and lazy, closed and then he gave a nod to his body guards. That's when I got nervous. Crap. Destry can't defend himself against them. They were huge. Nearly twice the size of him but did they have the skill Destry had?

Probably not.

"Come on, motherfucker!" Destry said, shoving the darker skinned one. "Hit me. Go ahead!"

The body guard looked to Silas. "Do you know who he is?"

Silas shrugged carelessly raising his drink to his lips. "Do you know who I am? I don't give a shit who he is."

Unfortunately for Silas, his bodyguards weren't as careless and backed up. They knew exactly who Destry was. "He's a world heavyweight boxing champion." The taller one said, trying to warn Silas. "I wouldn't—"

"Who fuckin' cares?" Silas shoved Destry's shoulder interrupting them. "Come on man, just leave. We're busy." His hand raised then, arching an eyebrow at Destry as he pushed his sweaty hair from his face. "Get the fucking hint and leave."

Destry laughed shaking his head as if a toddler had shoved him and stepped forward grabbing Silas by the shirt with both hands, his knuckles turning white. I was pushed back against the wall now, to my left was the exit but Destry and Silas were now blocking it. "You better kill me because I have *every* intention of killing *you*."

I hope he didn't mean that but something tells me he does.

He let go—giving him the opportunity—and Silas pulled his fist back and swung at Destry, which was the biggest mistake he'd ever made. Everything happened quickly, the glasses on the table crashing to the ground. I yelped as they collided, Destry's punches quick and absolutely no match for Silas. None. He was on the ground after two hits. I could see blood flowing from Silas' face, his body guards trying to get Destry off him. I was a little worried about Silas, only because I understood the power behind Destry's hits. He could kill someone if they weren't prepared. Fortunately for Silas, he was high.

Nothing was said, only punches delivered with such force you knew they were inflicting damage. When they finally did pull him off, Destry was bleeding, Silas having gotten in a punch or two but he looked at me with regretful eyes, on edge and raging. Commotion all around us took place and it was clear we needed to leave before the cops arrived. The bodyguards were pushing Destry away, ready to throw their own punches if necessary but they seemed to hold back. You'd think they would have put their own fear aside seeing how they were hired to protect Silas.

Silas started yelling, trying to collect himself and giving his bodyguards a verbal bashing over not protecting him. That's when I felt Destry's stare on me.

I wouldn't look at Destry, scared maybe, even though I could feel his eyes on mine, contrite and somewhat sincere. I didn't look because if I did, and found his eyes that I missed so much, I would no longer be dust I felt like when he found that article. I'd be lifeless because I knew how bad I hurt him.

His stare was challenging, incredulous even as he stared at Silas who was threatening to sue him for assault. It meant nothing to a guy like Destry.

"Fucking sue me, you piece of shit!" He growled turning away from him and then turned to me. "Come with me." He whispered, his voice strong, biting back so much.

When I didn't reply, his voice came stronger, his hand reaching out for me as the bodyguards helped Silas off the floor. "I'm not asking you, Tallan. Come with me right now."

"Why?"

His control was gone. He was pissed and more so than I'd seen in a while. It was the result of me. "Because. We need to talk and I'm not doing it in a fucking bar or around him."

We were out on the street now, a black truck with dark windows parked half on the street and half on the sidewalk. "Get in the truck." I knew then he wasn't asking me. He was demanding I go with him. There was no way I was staying here.

"Fine." I said, trying to appear casual. "Since you're asking so nicely."

My mind was racing with thoughts, from him, to Silas, to Marcus. At least I knew the truth now and the way it happened sucked. I'd spent years wondering and now I had the answer. One I'd never considered. But I had one.

I had no idea what Destry was about to say to me but I had a feeling it wasn't going to be good.

When I was inside the truck, he looked over at me. "Stay here. I'll be right back. Do not move."

His warning was so polite but there was no way I wanted to go in there anyway.

My thoughts raced again as to why he went back. I know the cops were called, surely we'd need to get out of here…and fast.

Chapter Seventeen
SUCKER PUNCH

An unexpected punch that catches a person completely off guard. The term sucker punch dates back to 1947 in the sport of boxing.

Destry returned to the truck ten minutes later, his breathing just as heavy as it was inside. I wanted to ask what he did but by the blood on his gray t-shirt that hadn't been there earlier, he got in another fight, or finished one.

The drive to his apartment was quiet, no music, nothing. Streets were empty, houses dark, and businesses closing down. At the stoplight, I snuck a peek at him, and his stare was forward, never yielding. Given his mood, I was nervous I had caused more drama he didn't need. I probably shouldn't have called him but I knew he was my only option.

Honestly, I needed to experience tonight. I had to. If I didn't, I would have never fully moved on from Silas. I would have constantly been wondering if there was still anything there between us.

With one hand on the wheel, Destry grabbed my purse from me, dug out my phone and looked for a number. When he found what he was looking for, he held the phone up to his ear.

"Jared? Yeah… it's me, Destry. I have Tallan… yeah… I'm takin' her back to my place… ok."

And then he hung up and tossed my phone back at me, never bothering to put it back in my purse. It landed on my lap and then fell onto the floorboard.

Like him, I made no attempt to retrieve it. Not only was I exhausted, physically and mentally, I was shaken. He parked in the parking garage below his building and turned off the ignition. "Jared said he'd come get you later."

"How did you know where I was?"

He didn't look at me as he spoke. Instead his eyes were on his keys in his hand. "I followed you."

That's all that was said before we got out.

The elevator doors slid open and we both walked in, silent. As soon as we were inside the elevator of his apartment building, I felt like I should rock back and forth. Cry until I had nothing left and then maybe I would be okay. But it was all bullshit. I wouldn't be okay because I had put myself in that position and let the one thing that I had overlooked get away. I looked at him then, my vision blurring.

"Why are you crying? You put yourself in that position." Shaking his head, he stared at his feet. "I fucking warned you that's all he wanted from you."

I wanted to say something snarky right then. But I had nothing. "I had to know."

He frowned and looked at me like he wanted to say something more. I waited—nothing. He swallowed, his eyes intense, maybe too intense. Feeling controlled, something flickered behind his eyes, but he blinked, and it was gone. And then, in typical Destry fashion, he laughed bitterly. "I hope it was worth it and you got the answers you needed."

"Fuck you." My voice seemed desperate for him to listen to me, though my words and my tone were clearly not insinuating my level of desperation, but he wasn't hearing any of it. Or maybe he couldn't listen to me. Maybe he still doesn't care enough to. Tears stung my throat.

There seemed to be a silent challenge between us. Destry didn't need to be loud to get his point across, though he could be at times, he did it in his own intuitive way. I knew, without a doubt, he was quick to stand up for himself.

Destry spread his arm, as if he was inviting me to, his voice thick with sarcasm I knew him well for. "Go ahead, baby."

"That's not what I meant, asshole." My voice was escalating again, my heart ready to beat out of my chest and throw itself on the ground before him.

He raised his eyebrows. "You call me to beat up pretty boy for you and *I'm the asshole?*"

In my mind, the conversation was far from over, but for Destry, it wasn't.

A scowl settled over his face as he crossed his arms over his chest when the elevator doors opened on the seventeenth floor. "There's the fucking door then." His words hit me leaving a sting against my skin.

I lost it. I was so pissed at him for acting this way when he didn't know the entire story. Or even wanted to know it. Would he even care at that point?

I looked at him so furiously hurt that he wouldn't listen that I was scared my voice would break and I wouldn't get out what I needed. I could have told him about Marcus right then. I could have.

I choked out a breath as another round of tears started. His intensity returned at the sight, his body stiffening.

He looked up at me then, his brow scrunched when I walked out of the elevator and down the hall to his apartment. I had no other place to go right then and felt safe with him, believe it or not. "You never planned on telling me, did you?"

"That's not true. I planned on telling you about the article. I did."

I don't know why but he truly seemed surprised and didn't say anything.

When we got inside Destry's apartment, he said nothing to me and my anger was starting to take over. He made me come here so he could treat me like shit. That's exactly what he was doing. Revenge. I slammed the door behind me, which got his attention. He looked back at me, and I smiled, trying that condescending one he was so good at.

Destry set his phone, keys, and wallet on the kitchen counter and then looked over at me again. "What's the matter, honey?" He was taunting me with the curve of his lips and the smirk that touched his eyes. He was being vindictive.

"Don't be an asshole, Destry." I threw my purse down, not caring if it spilled out, slamming the door shut with my foot. When I looked around his apartment, it was evident this last week hadn't been easy on him. Around twenty long necks were scattered around the living room along with a hole in the wall by his bedroom door confirmed it hadn't been easy. "I'm sorry I went there. I wasn't trying to upset you." I moved closer to him, but kept my distance. "I had to know."

"Yeah, I know." His irritation spoke in his stance and the way his eyes held mine as he paced the living room, his hands, red and swollen, clasped behind his head as though he was trying to control himself. He still hadn't calmed down. Before I had too much time to react, he stopped pacing and hovered over me, his eyes watchful of my reaction. "You made that perfectly clear. All you want is your story."

"I didn't mean it like that." I sighed, feeling like I was suffocating with him that close, that angry, and that defensive for something he didn't understand. Quickly, I brushed away the blame-worthy tears streaming down my face that I couldn't hide any longer and took a step back.

"But you did," Destry said, keeping his eyes on mine. His anger was flaring. That part I understood given how the night had unfolded. "You wrote that article. *My* story. That's a story. You went to him to get your answer. That's an ending to *your* story."

I was losing my patience with him. He brought me here to treat me like shit. "My God, you're so frustrating."

"Yeah, well ..." He finally stepped back creating a few inches of distance, his hands raised at me. "You're a bitch."

"I am not." I glared trying to let him know this wasn't exactly helping us move past this.

"Yep, you're a bitch."

"I know what you're doing. You're trying to push me away. Yeah, you came there to help me but you had no intention of giving me a chance to explain myself, did you?" I gave him a glare that went unnoticed.

"Shut up," he said, keeping his eyes locked with mine.

"Okay ..." I gave my own condescending smile. "Have it your way."

Destry pushed against my shoulder, and I fell against the couch. He smirked as he walked toward the balcony but added, "Finally."

I wasn't finished with our argument, though, and had a few things I needed to say, so I followed him. He sighed when I came outside. "Haven't had enough?"

I did what I thought was necessary for the situation. I kicked his shin. "Don't be a fucking jerk about this. And why are you acting like this?"

Destry's breath caught in his throat, his eyes immediately darkened and looked at me, the anger still heavy and oppressing in his tone. "Why not?"

"You don't even know what happened?"

"It was pretty fucking clear what happened in there if you ask me. But you know what, go ahead," he said, with another chuckle. "Tell me what he did so I can go back and kill him."

I wasn't laughing. I wasn't because I knew there was some seriousness to his threat. "That's not nice, Destry. You've got some serious anger issues. Don't act like you have some kind of vengeance against him."

"Whatever," he grunted, kicking his legs up onto the railing and leaning back in the plastic chair that was out there. Beside him I noticed a dozen empty beer cans scattered around. His swollen bloody hand rose to run the back of his hand of the cut on his cheek that Silas left. "I'm not angry. I'm just pissed off."

Like there's a difference.

"Fine, Destry, take me home then. If this is the way this shit is going to go, take me home. I don't want to be here."

"So what?" Destry snapped, jerking his legs from the balcony to sit a little straighter, his posture tense as he leaned forward with his elbows on his knees. "You fuckin' hate me now because I was trying to protect you from being raped by a fucking douchebag or being angry because you used me to write a story about me?"

"I wasn't going to be raped, Destry." Losing a little steam, I sat down beside him in the other chair next to his. "You're exaggerating."

He was quiet for a moment and I looked out over the city and the view he had of Elliott Bay.

"It sure as shit looked that way to me," he mumbled. "You're so fucking naïve. What the fuck did you expect when you went there? Did you think he just wanted to talk? He's a fucking rock star, Tallan."

"Why do you even care? You've made it perfectly clear you don't give a shit." I asked. "I don't need you to protect me. You're not my father."

"Yeah, sweetheart." He gave another scornful glare my way. He called me sweetheart just to pour salt in the wound his words left. "You can be goddamn sure I'm not your fucking dad. Why did you even call me?"

Just as I was about ready to walk away, he grabbed my hand when I stood, the fire in him simmering down slightly. "Tell me, why did you call me to rescue you? Why not Jared?"

I shrugged.

He let me walk away and gave me some space. In the twenty minutes he sat outside, his temper had calmed as did mine. I sat on his couch, still in my dress, ready to start crying again when I looked to my phone to see a missed call from Jared.

Destry came back in so I set my phone on the table.

"Why did you come then? If you don't care, why did you come?" The words hung in the air, apprehension suffocating me.

Destry picked up the beer on the coffee table, diverting his eyes from mine. He didn't make eye contact, and I knew why. After taking a drink, he set the bottle down, still no eye contact. His expression remained the same. His eyes focused on the ceiling when he finally sat down beside me. "I couldn't just leave you there."

"Why couldn't you have just read the article?" My words came out choked as the tears flowed again. He knew now that I was crying. There was no hiding it.

He looked at me, demanding truth. "Just be honest. You used me."

"No I didn't. I decided to write the article to help you. Deep down I knew you weren't who they said you were."

"You don't even know me."

"You're right… I don't. Because you wouldn't let me. I know the guy who treated me like shit and I know the one who fucked me. Two totally different people if you ask me."

"Tallan …" He grimaced. He couldn't look at me. "You look at that shit from my angle. *You* came to me looking for a personal trainer. *You* started asking questions. *You* asked me to fuck you. And you wrote that article and knew personal shit about me I hadn't told anyone else. How would that look to me?"

"But you didn't even read it."

Nothing was said for close to a minute. His palms pressed to his face, digging at his eyes, and then he groaned, dropping them beside him. "No. I didn't. And I still haven't. I won't."

"Why?"

"Why do you think?" I didn't like where this was going, and he knew it by the way his eyes wouldn't meet mine. "I don't care what it says. You broke my trust. You should have told me in the beginning you were writing it."

I should have done a lot differently. I shouldn't have trusted when Silas called me after five years. I should have been more curious as to why and how he got my number. Instead I was star-struck in a way. I should have been concerned when Marcus pushed me to write the article. I look for details for a living but yet I missed that one.

I also should have told Destry in the beginning.

My heart felt like a knife had been stabbed through it, and it was trying to beat around this foreign object, and this vital organ was simultaneously breaking in two, yet still trying to beat around the very thing that was ripping it apart. I felt guilty and rightfully so.

"I need to leave."

Destry shook his head. "No. You can't leave."

"Why not?"

"Because. I said so."

I intended on going into the bathroom to run some cold water over my face but then I stayed in there. I ran to his bathroom and slammed the door shut. Spent the entire night in there. Crying. It may have been weak but mustering any other type of emotion at this point was futile. I went after a man who was in my past, all the while forgetting about the man that was in my present and was sure to be my future, that is until I totally screwed everything up.

It was nearing morning, I assumed by the light coming in from the small window, when Destry pounded on the door. "Open the door. I have some things to say to you and I'm not going to say them to you while you're crying on my bathroom floor and there's a fucking door between us. Get out."

He's such a dick.

"Nah," I said, trying really hard to act like he hadn't ripped my heart out. It wasn't working though. "This works well for me. You should be used to distance, you know."

He surprised me, yet again, when his voice came louder, his hand hitting the door. "You wrote a fucking article about my life and our experience together. At least let me explain some things to you."

Hmmm. So he read it. Finally.

"Well, you better say it through the door. I'm not moving." I was more embarrassed than anything. No way did I want to face him right now. Sure, I wanted him to read it but now that he had, how would I face him?

"You better get up." He said, some amusement sparking in his tone. "I've never cleaned that floor. Imagine the germs on it and I can't completely say I've hit the mark every time I've used the toilet."

I nearly vomited. I'd spent the entire night crying on that floor.

He let me sleep on it? Bastard.

Just a second later, I was standing there before him while he leaned into the door frame with no shirt on.

See, he's just teasing me. I knew it.

"Put your shirt on." I demanded, as if I had any verbal power over this man, crossing my arms over my chest.

"No." He shook his head, flexing his muscles. Bastard.

I looked away. "Then I'm not talking to you."

"Why?" In amusement his eyebrows lifted.

"Because I can't focus when you don't have a shirt on."

"Fine. Take your dress off." Destry moved, shifting his stance and crossed his arms over his chest. "I can't focus."

"Why?" My eyes lingered over his chest muscles.

Jesus, why do you have to be so sexy?

I expected him to say something, anything, but there was only silence, the awkward kind before his eyes deceived him and he briefly looked at me. "Because you wore it for him. Not me. Take it off."

I did. Right there in the hallway leaving me in my bra and underwear. He didn't like that one bit. Well, he did, obviously, but it was clearly a distraction he didn't want right then. Disappearing into his bedroom, a drawer slammed shut and he returned with two t-shits, handing me one and keeping one for himself.

So there I was sitting on his couch, both of us wearing his t-shirts. I'd finally stopped crying and he had the article in his hand, I had a bottle of vodka in mine drinking it straight up. It was seven that morning and we were both drinking. Pathetic.

He held up the article standing in front of me. "Did you write this for you, or me?"

I considered that for a moment. "A little of both."

"Why?"

He sat down beside me, our shoulders touched, and he sighed. "Because I think the public, including me, has the wrong image of you."

His eyes met mine. There was an uncertainty in his stare. "Maybe they have the right one."

"I don't believe that." I couldn't break away from his eyes.

Destry took a deep breath before continuing, and even though his voice was soft, I could hear the embarrassment in his words. "I threw that fight on purpose." The intensity in his eyes returned.

"Why?"

His hand came up to run along his jaw, his eyes narrowing at the wall. He shook his head, contemplating his response. "For her."

"And then she left you?"

He nodded and set the article down. "And then she left me."

My eyes, red and spilling over with tears, met his. The guilt tugged at my gut. I wasn't any better than her. "I'm sorry."

"It's not your fault. I just… think if you're going to have an image of me," His eyes found mine again. "I want you of all people to have the right one."

Tentatively I reached out and touched his shoulder. "I knew when I saw you sparring for the first time you didn't lose that fight because he was better. There was no way a man with your speed, skill and style could have lost."

He nodded but didn't say anything.

"Do you regret it?"

Destry leaned forward and retrieved his beer. He looked at the bottle in his hand, tipping it with a contemplative glare. "I do. I said he was a better fighter. He wasn't. And I'm done fighting for them. It used to be something I enjoyed. I've always wanted to be a heavyweight champion. Never anything else. Then one day I lost that and I started doing it for money. I lost my mind doing it that way. I was the champion of the world and lost it for her. I want that back."

"Her or the title?"

"The title."

I gave him a nod. "Then get it back."

"I plan to."

We didn't say anything for a few minutes, when he nudged my shoulder with his. His hands were restless, searching for himself within all this.

I blinked slowly, the sight of him being so vulnerable nearly bringing me to tears.

His eyebrows rose, and he looked at me out of the corner of his eyes. "Did you fuck him?"

I didn't answer. I didn't feel like I needed to. He should have known the answer to that.

"I don't like it when I ask a question and don't get an answer." He reached over and touched my cheek angling my face towards his. "Did you fuck him?"

"What do you think the answer to that question is?"

"I don't know. I thought I knew you… but I'm not so sure anymore."

"No." There was some anger to my tone.

"Do you regret it?" His voice sounded sincere. Like he's honestly asking.

"Going to see the concert?"

"No." He said quietly, almost timid. Seeing him this way made me nervous. "After everything… do you regret sleeping with me?"

"No. I don't at all. I didn't then and I still don't." I repeated, knowing he'd already asked me that. "I hate that you thought I would sleep with Silas." My eyes dropped to my hands wrapped around the coffee mug. "Especially after the way we were."

Destry hung his head in shame. "I'm sorry. But what did you expect me to think? When we talked about you going to that concert… you made is seem like you wanted that to happen."

"After everything that happened between us, did you really think I would have done that?"

"No … I didn't want to think that way… but my judgment has been clouded the past six weeks."

I had to admit, I smiled right then. I had this effect over this mountain of a man. Little ol' me could make him do things that six weeks ago he wouldn't have even thought of. Oh yeah, who's to say that power only resides in the male physique?

But then I had to ask the question I'd been dying to know the answer to, probably more than I wanted to know the answer to why Silas left.

"Why did you sleep with me that night and then tell me you knew about that article? Why not just tell me?"

He was quiet for a long moment and then looked over at me. "I knew what would happen when I told you. I knew it was over when I found out, but, I couldn't let you go that easily."

"Why?"

"Because you were the first girl who didn't care who I was. Being champion didn't matter. What *we* had mattered. Or so I thought. And it wasn't easy to see any other way. I wanted to believe we had something that only we shared."

I considered that. "So how come you couldn't see that I never meant to hurt you?"

"I don't know." He shrugged. "I just couldn't. I'm still a guy...I can be very single minded at times."

"How did you find out?"

"Adam warned me. Then I went to see my dad and saw your name on the sign-in sheet. I did some research and then I saw you having lunch with Marcus Hadley. I remembered him and then Adam reminded me of who he was." He sounded sad as he spoke. "Then I found your notebook when you were in the bathroom at the gym, it fell out of your bag when I moved it off the weight bench"

In a sense, it was like I felt guilty for everything, as if somehow I had something to do with it, but I didn't. I never would have done something like this had Marcus not pushed me to do so.

And with Destry, I hurt him. Badly. More than he wanted to admit. That was on me.

He wasn't going to forgive me right away or forget what happened, but was it even something that needed to be forgiven?

No. I needed to show him he could trust me.

When you made a mistake you were usually harder on yourself than anyone else. I tortured myself over it. Destry knew that.

It wasn't about forgiveness. It was about our future and where we would take it, if we wanted it, if we had a future together.

I remembered when I asked myself why people lived for right now. I wanted one night. I got it. What if you could have the greatest love of your life, but you had to relive the past to find it again?

Well, I went back to the beginning and found that love. Where I ended up was far from where I thought I would be. I no longer wanted that love.

Where I was now was where I should have been all along.

This was it. This was what mattered.

I used to hear girls say they'd never forget their first love. Even Jared said that.

When you think about it, it's the first piece of your heart that you gave to someone else. When you're young, the love you gave your parents was different. They were there from the beginning. You automatically loved them from the start; you were designed to. Then someone, your first love, came along and you gave your heart to him or her. The difference was you gave it. Or maybe they stole it.

Think about when you tie your shoes in a knot. When I was little, I used to tie my shoes in double, even triple, knots so they wouldn't come untied when I was running around. Then night would come, and I'd have to untie them. Those second and third knots were always easy to get untangled, but that first knot, the strongest one, always gave me the most trouble.

That was first love. A bond you couldn't untie. Eventually, if you were strong enough, you could get it untied and move on.

Surely you survived, but wasn't always easy.

My theory?

Move on and buy new laces.

Chapter Eighteen
SOUTHPAW

Southpaws are left handed fighters (unorthodox). They put their right foot forward, jab with their right hand and throw power punches with their left hand (rear hand). To a "normal" right handed fighter a southpaw's punches are coming from the wrong side. When a right handed and left handed boxer fight each other their lead foot is almost on top of the other person's. Southpaws aren't always born left handed some are converted southpaws.

Thursday
May 19, 2011

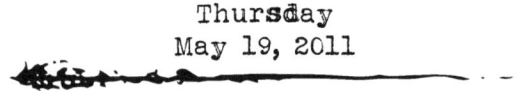

I could walk away and deep down I would be as fine as I was the day I met Destry. But would I be happy if I walked away right now? No. I don't think I would be.

I learned a few things since I met him. Sometimes I felt like a breath was never really a breath but a shallow passing of air, a gasp needing relief. I felt like there was a wall in my lungs, which prevented them from expanding. Meeting him and experiencing what I did these last six weeks had changed me completely.

We had just finished eating take-out when Destry said possibly the most sincere words yet. Ones that I knew he feared.

"You're never gonna see me as Destry." He said, keeping his eyes low. "You'll always see a trainer, a fighter. Never me."

"You're wrong, Destry." I put my plate on the coffee table. "It's all I've ever seen."

He was looking at me again. I couldn't deal with the vulnerable side of him; it made me feel vulnerable, too.

"Tell me what you want, Tallan. Do you want me to walk away?" he asked, stepping forward as we stood in his kitchen now cleaning up. "Tell me." He reached out and cupped my face. Bending down, in true Destry style of just going for it, he lowered his lips to mine, pressing lightly, warm and soft. My reaction was anything but gentle. And then neither was his. He inhaled loudly, my breath in my lungs exhaling just as harshly.

"The way I feel about you hasn't changed." I said against his lips. "It never will."

He pulled away watching my reaction. "No, that's not good enough. You have to say it. If you want me to walk away, then say it."

This was what mattered. The experience. The forgiveness and how it made you feel. You rarely realized what forgiveness could do for your soul. But really, it was your love that really mattered. It was the only thing that mattered, aside from the experience.

This was us forgiving in our own way.

"Everyone who has ever said 'trust me' has left me with nothing." His eyes when he looked at me, they wrecked me completely. "Are you gonna do the same?"

My voice shook when I spoke. A familiar ache started in my chest and weaved around my throat. "No."

"You see me, right?" his bloodshot eyes found mine. "You see who I am now, all fight and no faith. If you leave, if I can't trust you, what will happen then?"

"You can trust me." I reached out to touch the stubble of his jaw, my palm flattening against his cheek.

"I'm not going anywhere. My dad once told me while he was training for a fight against Salvador Reyner that a moment of pain is worth a lifetime of glory. I believe that now."

I sighed, smiling at him as there was a knock on his door. "Do you feel that?" he placed my hand over his chest ignoring the knocking.

"Yeah?"

"It's a heartbeat. That's all I've had to tell me I'm alive this past year. A beat. And then you came around. You made me feel something pure, something worth believing."

"I love you." I breathed, feeling like I've never felt before.

Oh God, I said it. I fucking said it!

He smiled and touched my cheek. "I'll fight for you." I remember his earlier words, "I fight for who I love."

He looked at me wearily. His eyes shifted from mine to my body and hands, searching my face for answers. I did the same, only his didn't offer anything but the evidence of a rough night.

Now here we were. Two hearts, two souls, one outcome.

You could guess where it led from there.

Yeah. The bedroom. I would think that was the direction we shouldn't go. It wasn't healthy, right?

I didn't care. This was our forgiveness.

His strong hands trailed over my body, and then his voice brought me back to his face.

"Tell me you love me," he panted, shifting his position to look at me. "Tell me again."

He kicked away the remaining barriers of clothing dragging me to the middle of his bed, my head supported as he lowered me to the mattress. His knee was between my thighs, tongue between my lips, my hands greedy as they slid over his back muscles and squeezed his shoulders in an attempt to bring him closer.

Shaking his head, his hands moved over my body, then lower to my hips as he sat back on his feet and then pushed himself down my body.

Oh God, I knew what he was doing.

Destry sighed taking in my naked body. "It fucking hurt to think I'd never see this again."

I ran my hands through his hair when he curled his hands around my thighs and spread them for him. "I couldn't agree more." I moaned. "It was torture."

When he kissed the inside of my thigh, I got a little nervous.

"You don't have to…"

He shook his head moving his kiss to my center, pulling back slightly, his tongue swept over his lower lip. "I wasn't asking for your approval, Tallan." His voice took on a quiet intensity.

Pussy. Meet your soul mate.

I clawed at him, clutching at his strong arms, his tongue lapped at me from my clit all the way to my ass, his fingers hard and insistent in all the right areas. It was a reminder of the shower and I moaned at how good it felt and the shivers it sent through my body. He made me feel like every nerve ending in my body was on fire when he was around.

After my first orgasm, Destry pulled back and watched me coming down from the high.

"Fuck me, Destry. Please…"

"Do you know what you're asking for?" His look was long and hard, our loud breathing filled the room as his hands rested on either side of my head, and he pushed forward. His knees spread my legs; each movement was slow and so good.

"I do."

"You can still leave. I won't make you stay if you don't want to."

He pressed his chest closer, warm skin comforting. I missed that warmth so much. It was then that he whispered that he never wanted to stop, and I whimpered refusing to allow any space between us.

"I'm not going anywhere."

"Fuck," he breathed, his nose brushing mine as he traced my bottom lip with his tongue, as if he was having trouble holding back for another second. "I've missed you so much."

He raised himself, hands fisted in the sheets and pushed forward. My eyes found his, bright with desire but clouded with lust I knew. My fingertips grazed over his flushed cheeks and then over his shoulders and to his sides. My nails dug into his sides, while I kissed from chin to temple and back as he cradled my head. My eyes drifted closed and took everything he was giving me. I didn't realize how much I'd missed this until right now.

I pushed back and guided my palm to his heart, keeping my eyes locked with his.

"Let this be mine," I pleaded. His eyes blinked heavy, and my words were low. "Please."

He took my bottom lip between his teeth before pushing forward one last time, a low moan trapped against skin.

"It *is* yours, Tallan," he murmured against my chest. "That will never change. Never."

I wrapped my arms around his neck bringing him back to me, slick bodies meeting their limit.

"Don't ever leave me again," he said, staring at me, holding my gaze with a fire that was still present. His hips grinding into mine faster. I could feel his balls slapping against me, my head being pushed up into his headboard as he exposed every little piece of my soul.

When he started to move more forceful, I remembered his strength and how much I craved it. I wanted to tell him to pull my hair, but I didn't. I'd let him move at his own pace.

The way he watched me, scrutinizing every breath and every blink assured me there was no bitterness there anymore. He didn't hate me for what I did, he loved with every piece of himself that he gave to me. This was him forgiving me. I could feel it then presented in his warmth and gentle touch.

I heard myself make a low moan when one of his hands traced down my chest over my waist and then gripped me firmly as he pressed his pelvis into me a little harder. "You wanted it… take it." He growled grinding his hips into mine.

I would. I would forever take it for this man.

He gave me more right then. He gave me as much as I wanted, everything I needed. And I took it all.

My right hand traced his face, slid down his neck, his arm, over his collarbone and gently over the rippled muscles of his chest. The touch of his bare skin with mine was everything I needed.

With the need, we didn't last long at all and it was over sooner than both of us wanted.

When his breath evened out he rolled off me and to my side holding me against him.

He whispered in my ear, low and raspy, rocking forward. "I love you."

"I love you too." I said meaning every word of it.

That night, just as I was contemplating staying over again, this time in his bed and not on the floor in his bathroom, Jared called my phone. I answered knowing he wasn't going to stop calling.

"Where have you been?"

"With Destry." I looked over at Destry who was staring at the ceiling as I sat on his bed with him. His left hand raised and ran down my spine. I smiled, content with how this was going and how easy it seemed for us to forgive.

"I was just there and no one answered. I'm coming over there, with Marcus." And then he hung up.

Immediately I was fuming as I started throwing clothes on. Destry pulled his shirt over his shoulders. "What's wrong?"

For a short time, I'd forgotten all about Marcus. Now just the thought made me angry, my cheeks flushed as my blood started to boil. "Jared is coming over with Marcus."

His body tensed immediately. "Marcus Hadley?"

Oh God, I forgot… they knew one another. Well, if Destry didn't kill him, I would.

"Yes."

"Why the fuck would he do that?" His anger was menacing.

"Well, they're friends… and Marcus was probably worried I found out about his lie."

"What lie?"

I drew in a deep breath and reached for a pair of Destry's sweatpants. "He called Silas and convinced him to meet me. I've known Marcus since high school, he knew Silas too, and I had told him one night how I wished I could see Silas again. Silas never called because he wanted to see me. He thought I wanted to see him."

There was a knock at the door and I couldn't explain much before I was flying at Marcus like a spider monkey. "You motherfucker!"

Marcus tried to shield me, his hands defending himself as we crashed against the wall outside Destry's apartment. "I'm sorry."

Destry grabbed me and hauled me back inside his apartment, Jared and Marcus followed.

"I'm really sorry, Tallan." He glanced at Destry, his eyes wide and panicked. "I'm sorry to both of you."

"Not good enough!" I twisted from Destry's embrace and made sure my footing was correct and I drew my right fist back and practiced that right hook I was taught.

Nailed it. Fucking nailed it. And might have broken my hand. Destry had forgot to tell me how bad that hurt.

Jared looked at Marcus and then me. Destry who was standing there smiling now, was still moments away from hitting Marcus himself. "Nicely done, tough girl."

"I think I broke my hand." I curled myself into Destry, whimpering like a baby. He wrapped his arm around me

"What's going on?" Jared asked, helping Marcus. I barely did any damage but his nose was bleeding so I was satisfied with that.

I twisted slightly from Destry's embrace to stare at Jared. "That fucking douche bag used me! He called Silas and gave him my number. Told him to call me."

"Okay…" Jared scratched the side of his head. It was hard for him to follow along sometimes.

"You're a bad cop." I shoved him. "Who told you about Destry, Jared?" I glared at Marcus who hung his head.

"Well, Marcus did at poker the night after Silas called you."

"Exactly! He knew I would do anything to look good for Silas! Who he called, and told to get in touch with me because he knew I wanted to see him. And then he knew I wanted to lose weight, and he wanted his story he couldn't get so he used me to get it."

It took Jared another minute before it dawned on him.

Destry growled behind me, his patience gone. "You better get out of my fucking apartment right now." He said to Marcus stepping towards him.

Marcus scrambled knowing Destry's punches were a hell of a lot stronger than mine.

"Oh my God!" Jared shook his head as Marcus stepped past him and out the door. Jared followed him, no doubt ready to kick his friend's ass. "Why the fuck would you do that to her? Get back here!" Marcus started to run from him. "I'm going to arrest you!"

I would have stood there for hours fighting with Marcus trying to get every detail out of him about why he did it. Marcus was a reporter. He'd do anything for a story and when he couldn't get it, he used his resources. In reality, was I any different?

I was about to follow Marcus, because that didn't stop me from feeling pissed, when Destry caught me and slammed the door shut. "I'm pissed right now. And I want to kill that guy but I need to do something. Right now. I can't wait any longer and let the chance slip away." He leaned down and took my swollen red hand in his kissing my knuckles softly.

"What?" he backed me up against the door pressing his body against mine, so strong, so firm and exactly what I needed.

"Will you go on a date with me? As my girlfriend? None of this fucking around shit anymore. I'm yours. And you're mine."

"Are you asking me out?" Internally all that anger was suddenly gone. I no longer felt that pain in my hand.

"Yes. I am." He smiled leaning in to kiss me once, and then pulling back. "Jared said I could."

"You asked him?" I shook my head knowing what Jared said. Or at least what he would have said.

He nodded. "I did."

"And he said?"

"He said you two have an arranged marriage but that I could borrow you for a while."

I shook my head pulling his lips to mine. "He's lying."

"I'm sure." He grinned leaning in to kiss me.

"I was granted a re-match for December twenty-fourth."

My hands immediately covered my mouth, not only did I have a mouthful of quite possibly the best steak in the world, but I couldn't believe what Destry had just told me. "Are you serious?"

He nodded lifting his wine glass to his lips. "I am."

I stared at him. This was our first official date. He'd taken me to Metropolitan Grill and it was the first time we'd ever been dressed up together too. He was wearing a dark gray dress shirt, black tie and slacks. I was wearing a dark gray dress that clung to my every curve. It didn't matter that I never ended up losing the entire twenty pounds. What mattered was that I was comfortable and I had closure. Destry had opened my eyes to so much more than I ever could have imagined in just six weeks.

Since last night, Destry and I hadn't left his bed. Until now. When he decided he was taking me on that date. We were both ignoring reality. I had a handful of messages from Jared, as did Destry. Neither one of us wanted to face the real world. We wanted right now. A moment where it was just us, for just one night. I knew eventually I would need to sort out so much but it didn't matter right then. Finally I was living for right now and that made perfect sense to me.

"So you start training then?" I set my wine glass down on the table and cut another small chunk off my steak.

"I've been training since the day I lost. I never stopped."

I watched his features as he chewed slowly, the dim lighting over the restaurant casting shadows over his eyes but I still saw the intensity behind them. With a man like Destry, it just didn't make sense to me that he threw that fight.

"Why did you throw that fight, I know it wasn't just about Stella, what really happened?"

Destry stopped chewing mid bite, his eyes snapped to mine like he wasn't expecting that question from me. I never thought I'd ask it. That was his business. If he wanted to tell me, he would. Drawing in a deep breath, he leaned back in his chair. "Stella and I had been fighting non-stop. About everything too. Didn't matter what. I was in the middle of training for the fight and it's hard to give your attention to anything but training. You have to stay focused. Usually she understood but this time... she didn't. She said she was leaving two weeks before the fight. I begged her to stay. I couldn't have her leave. It was right after my dad had his stroke. I thought for sure if she left too, I'd have no one." Raising his right hand, he ran it over his jaw. "She said, if I loved her, I'd throw the fight and prove it. Prove to her that she meant more than boxing did to me." He shrugged. "So I did. And it was the stupidest thing I've ever done because she left me anyway. With Ray. She had been seeing him all along. Now knowing that she'd been with Ray the entire time, I swear that I think that bitch must have bet a shitload of money against me. No doubt in my mind."

My heart hurt for him. Tears rolled down my face and he leaned forward to wipe them away.

"I didn't tell you any of that to make you feel bad for me. I did that. It's on me and no one else."

"What happened after that?" I wanted to understand Destry and everything he had been through. I wanted to understand where all that hate came from. The problem was that it was never hate that Destry had. It was too much passion. It was too strong for anyone to see.

Pulling his hand back, he paused and took another drink of his wine. Slowly his eyes met mine. "Well, she left and the next day Danny told me he'd bet on that fight for me to win. He bet the bar. So I got it back for him and started doing some training around town to make some money. Everything I had went into getting the bar back and taking care of my dad."

"How did you... so you thought you'd train some fat girl to get into shape?" I laughed at the irony of how this all happened.

"You were never fat. You were unbelievably sexy." He said, his stare intent on mine. I believed him too. "Danny had said he had a friend who needed some help. He never told me it was a woman so when you showed up, I was a little confused but went with it because you were hot. Then I stared at you the entire time, hormones got in the way and then I had sex with you. I was done after that." He laughed, that laugh that was so cute.

"Well, I thought you were the world's biggest asshole," I leaned in giving him a nice view down the front of my dress. Naturally his eyes lowered. "But I'm glad we got drunk that night."

"We weren't *that* drunk."

I winked for a change. "No. We weren't."

We continued to eat our meals, flirting, touching under the table like all first dates might when Destry got a confused look on his face. "I still don't understand why Marcus would have called Silas. Why did that matter if he wanted the story on me?"

"Marcus and I had talked about Silas many times since high school. I said I wanted to see him and he knew I had concerns about my weight. Somehow he knew that you were a personal trainer and worked up his plan from there."

Destry seemed deep in thought and then shook his head. "I… I'm not the easiest person to get along with… and I make a lot of mistakes on the boyfriend front."

"Are you trying to scare me?" I laughed as I slipped off my shoes and ran my foot along the inside of his thigh seductively.

"Yes. I just want you to be prepared for being with a fighter."

My foot reached his lap and traced the outline of the hardness that had formed from me running my foot up his thigh. "I think I'm prepared for anything. I had a good trainer."

Quirking an eyebrow at me, amused maybe, Destry grabbed my foot under the table and then slid his hips forward pressing his erection into my foot. "Have you ever been fucked, baby?"

Shivering under the heat of his eyes, I leaned forward again, my breath blowing over his face. "Show me what you got, fighter."

We were just about to leave, Destry was paying for our meals, when Jared came into the restaurant wearing his uniform with another officer to his left. He looked all business, which seemed unusual for him.

Shuffling through the tables and many stares, they both stopped at our table.

Destry finished signing the credit card receipt and gave me a nod, as if he was silently telling me everything was fine.

"Jared…" I looked up at him. "What's going on?"

He blinked slowly, but said nothing, only spared me with a brief glance.

The officer beside him turned to Destry with handcuffs in hand. "Destry Stone?"

Destry nodded, his apprehensive stare moving from Jared to the officer that spoke to him. "You're under arrest for the murder of Silas Cade."

Coming February 2015

217

"The fight is won or lost far away from witnesses — behind the lines, in the gym, and out there on the road, long before I dance under those lights."

Muhammad Ali

Acknowledgements

Thank you to everyone who continues to support me and my dream of writing. For the past year I've done nothing but write Racing on the Edge. And then I ventured out of my comfort for the first time with All I Have Left. That got my motivation back to write outside of the family I know so well. Now I've gone a step further with The Trainer.

The bloggers who give me shout-outs, and the authors for being there for me. I would name all of you but that always seems to give them unwanted attention. They know who they are.

The Boy and Honey Girl, my world is you two. And I know you know that already but please never forget that.

I do have to thank the Gearheads and Shey's Shit Show. You're there for me no matter what. Elaine, Shanna, Erin, Megan, Marisa, Linda, Barb, and Janet, you girls keep me going every day. Love you!

About the Author

Shey Stahl is the author of the *Racing on the Edge Series, Waiting for You, Everything Changes, Delayed Penalty, All I have Left* and *The Trainer*. She enjoys spending time with her family at the local dirt tracks of the Northwest. You can follow her on the links below.

Facebook: https://www.facebook.com/shey.stahl.9
Website: www.sheystahl.com

Made in the USA
Charleston, SC
27 November 2014